Diamonds on the Danube

A River Cruise Novel

CHERYL DOUGAN

 FriesenPress

Suite 300 - 990 Fort St
Victoria, BC, V8V 3K2
Canada

www.friesenpress.com

ISBN
978-1-5255-8094-9 (Hardcover)
978-1-5255-8095-6 (Paperback)
978-1-5255-8096-3 (eBook)

1. *FICTION, MYSTERY & DETECTIVE, COZY*

Distributed to the trade by The Ingram Book Company

Diamonds on the Danube

Chapter One

Budapest

Adelle gazed out at the Danube from her stateroom window, tingling with excitement. She couldn't believe she was on a ship, docked in the heart of Budapest. As the river swirled past, glinting in the mid-afternoon sun, she admired the large castle-like fortress high on the opposite bank. She slid the floor-to-ceiling glass door open and breathed deeply.

How lucky can a grandma get? Adelle thought. She was looking forward to meeting new people, seeing new places, and experiencing new cultures. Let the river cruise begin!

Bang!

Startled, Adelle whirled around and saw the door vibrate off the wall. A younger, taller, and slimmer woman stood in the door frame, feet apart, hands on her hips, eyes blazing. Adelle estimated her to be around thirty.

"Who are you?" the woman demanded. "Why are you in my cabin?"

What? Adelle went rigid with fear. Her first instinct was to run but her path was blocked. She closed her eyes.

Breathe in, two, three, four.

Hold, two, three, four.

Breathe out, two, three, four.

Calmer, Adelle opened her eyes. The hostile blonde was still glaring at her. "Well?" she demanded.

Adelle consciously rolled her shoulders, then wiggled her fingers. "You must be Barb, my assigned cabin mate," she stammered.

"Wrong and wrong again. It's 'Barbara' and I am definitely not your 'mate.'"

Whoa. This wasn't starting out very well.

"Well?" Barbara demanded again. "Who are you?"

"I'm Adelle, your tour host."

"Tour host? What tour?"

Adelle was confused. Surely, her friend Maureen had updated Barbara about the tour. Obviously not. No wonder she's angry at finding a stranger in her room. Maureen owned a travel agency and had organized this trip for women who didn't want to travel alone. When she had asked Adelle last-minute to fill in as a tour host, the timing was perfect. Adelle was bored with retirement and had jumped at the opportunity.

"Didn't Maureen get in touch with you before you left?"

Barbara whipped out her phone, thumbed the screen repeatedly, then stopped. She slumped down onto the bed.

"Emergency gall bladder surgery," she mumbled.

Adelle felt sorry for Barbara. She was obviously very disappointed. "Maybe I should leave and let you get settled in."

Barbara stood up abruptly and closed the sliding glass door. "I get this bed," she declared, pointing to the single bed nearest the view.

Adelle sighed. *So much for watching the world drift by.* Then she brightened up. She probably wouldn't spend much time in the cabin anyway. "No problem," she said, as she transferred her carry-on luggage to the other bed. "I'm meeting the other three women—"

"Other women?" Barbara asked. She looked at her phone again. "Oh … a group."

"We're meeting on the deck for a late lunch," Adelle said. "Would you like to join us?"

"No," Barbara said curtly. "I have work to do." She turned back to the window.

I guess I've been dismissed. Adelle left, dodging a backpack and large rolling suitcase with a nylon briefcase attached to its extended handle.

Three pieces of luggage? How much could Barbara possibly need?

Adelle spotted Debbie and Tilly, the sisters from rural Saskatchewan, sitting at the table alongside the railing at the front of the ship. Debbie bounced to her feet. "Here we are," she sang, as she waved merrily. Adelle couldn't help smiling. Debbie's curly blonde hair was struggling to escape her bright pink head scarf as the sun glistened off her sparkly designer sunglasses. Tilly sat quietly, hands in her lap. Was she wearing clip-on sunglasses? Adelle didn't know those still existed.

"So, this is what 'al fresco dining' means," Tilly said, returning to the table with soup and a sandwich. "It's like eating off the tailgate of the truck when we're in the field, only with a fancy name."

"No tailgates here," Debbie said happily. "Someone else is doing the menu planning, gathering the food, cooking it, serving it, and cleaning up afterward."

"Some of us happen to like doing that," Tilly said, putting down her spoon. "I'm not hungry anymore. I'm going for a nap."

Somebody's grumpy, thought Adelle. This adventure was going to be more difficult than she had expected.

"Don't worry about her," Debbie reassured Adelle as Tilly stomped off. "My sister gets a little cranky when she's overtired." Debbie stabbed an olive from Tilly's plate, just as the last member of their group sat down at their table.

"Sorry I'm late," Teresa said, sliding her sunglasses down over her vibrant green eyes. Her shoulder-length auburn hair shone in the sunlight.

Adelle instinctively reached up to tuck any errant gray hair behind her ears, wishing she had squeezed in a hair appointment before the trip. That was the trouble with short hair—it always needed to be cut.

"It's so nice to eat outside," Teresa said. "This view is stunning."

The ship was docked between two bridges in the center of Budapest. The hills across the Danube were dotted with fortresses and church spires peeking out through the autumn foliage.

"I love our cabin," Debbie said.

Teresa agreed. "Did you notice how they've thought of everything? Storage room under the beds ..."

"The makeup counter ..." Debbie added.

"That doubles as a desk," Teresa said, and smiled. "The space is limited yet functional and serene at the same time. This ship reminds me of a floating boutique hotel."

Adelle sat back and relaxed in the warm sunshine as the women's voices blended into the sounds of the river flowing past.

"Adelle?"

Debbie was smiling at her. "We asked if you wanted to go shopping with us."

Shopping? She would rather visit the dentist! "Sorry, I guess I was daydreaming."

"Maybe you need to go for a nap, too," Debbie suggested with a friendly grin.

Good idea, Adelle thought. Then she remembered that Barbara was working in their room. No nap. But speaking of working, it was time to go and find the program director. She told Debbie and Teresa that she had a meeting and wished them fun shopping. Better them than her!

At dinner in the ship's main dining room, Teresa and Debbie shared their afternoon discovery of Budapest's Great Market Hall.

"It's a large indoor market," Debbie explained.

"Built in 1897," Teresa added.

Debbie was impressed with all the different vendors. There were fishmongers and butchers in the basement; produce stands, spices, and paprika vendors on the main level; and handicrafts, fine linens, and Hungarian food stalls on the top level.

"I'll bet Debbie handled every single item," Tilly said.

"Hello, pot," Debbie shot back, grinning at her sister.

Adelle briefly regretted not going on the walk; however, she had enjoyed meeting Lee, the ship's program director. He was easy to look at and talk to, and had laughed when she confessed that her meeting was an excuse to avoid shopping.

"Has Barb arrived yet?" Teresa asked, setting down her menu.

"You mean Barbara," Adelle replied, remembering her second confrontation with the young woman after lunch. As Adelle was leaving Lee's office, thanking him for being her alibi, she had collided with Barbara in his doorway. Adelle tried to apologize, but Barbara pointedly ignored her.

Strike three had happened just before dinner. Adelle had quietly opened their cabin door and tiptoed in. Barbara was propped against her headboard, hunched over her laptop. She had changed into an oversized gray sweatshirt, tattered jeans, and fuzzy blue-and-white striped socks. She kept flicking a loose strand of blonde hair out of her way.

"Hi," Adelle said quietly.

Barbara shot up and slammed her laptop closed. She glared at Adelle, blue eyes flashing. "You scared me," she cried.

"Sorry," Adelle said. "I came back to get ready for dinner."

Barbara pointed at the closet. "Your bag is in there." She continued to glare at Adelle. "Is that all you brought?"

Adelle explained that she traveled light, managing with only carry-on luggage. Even if her friends didn't believe her. They could do it too if they left their oversize jewelry, matching purses and shoes for every occasion, designer shampoo and conditioner, enough makeup for the year, at home. All that makeup, just to get the natural look. Adelle didn't understand them. Adelle knew she was babbling but she couldn't stop. Barbara made her so nervous.

She took a deep breath. "Are you joining us for dinner tonight?"

"Affirmative." Barbara had turned her back to Adelle and opened her laptop.

Adelle came back to the present and told Teresa that yes, Barbara was planning to join them for dinner.

Just when Adelle thought Barbara had forgotten about dinner, she saw her standing uncertainly in the doorway. Thank goodness, she had changed into casual black slacks and a light blue sweater set. She looked much prettier and friendlier without that sloppy ponytail.

Adelle waved Barbara over to their table and introduced her to Teresa and the sisters.

"Nice to meet you," Barbara said, smiling as she extended her hand.

Could this be the same girl? Adelle wondered. Polite? Charming? Maybe they could be friends after all.

Dinner was everything Adelle hoped it would be. Delicious food, excellent service, and stimulating conversation as the women got to know each other.

"Tilly, do you speak Hungarian?" Adelle asked as they waited for dessert to be served.

"A little."

"What did you say to the van driver on the way from the airport to the ship?" Adelle asked, wondering why the young man had flushed deep crimson from his collar to his cap.

"This should be interesting." Debbie chuckled. "Tilly, should we ask our waiter to translate?"

"Why not?" Tilly replied, sitting up taller.

Tilly repeated to their waiter what she had said to the van driver. He raised one eyebrow, looked away for a moment, and then grinned.

"What did she say this time?" Debbie asked.

"She told him to meet her behind the barn later," the waiter replied.

Everyone turned to Tilly. She blushed and then burst out laughing. Soon everyone was laughing with her.

"Another Tilly classic!" Debbie exclaimed.

Tilly struggled to regain her composure. "In Grade six, I had a crush on Hugo. He was a newcomer and was learning English. He was so cute." She looked dreamily out the dining room window before continuing. "I didn't know how to start a conversation with him, so I asked his older brother for help." Tilly started giggling again. "No wonder Hugo ran away every time he saw me!"

"My sister loves to learn languages," Debbie said. "It's how she meets men."

"She's just kidding." Tilly sat up tall again. "Learning languages is good for your brain and keeps you young."

"And interesting," Debbie teased. "The stories I could tell …"

Adelle was running for her life, being chased by barking dogs. "Stop, stop," she heard someone yelling. With a start, she recognized her own voice and woke up.

Where was she? Where were the yappy dogs? She pulled her covers up tightly under her chin, protecting herself from …

"Are you okay?" she heard in the darkness.

"Who are you?"

"Barbara, remember?"

A light snapped on. Adelle turned and saw Barbara staring at her from the other single bed.

Breathing in and out slowly, Adelle calmed her racing heart. "Sorry, I guess I was having a bad dream."

Barbara's eyes narrowed and she smiled thinly. "Maybe a coffee would help."

How thoughtful! "Yes, that would be nice."

"Good," Barbara said brusquely. "I take mine one-third regular, two-thirds decaf, and lots of milk. Hot milk."

Snap. The room went dark again.

What? Was Adelle still dreaming? Did Barbara actually expect her to go and get coffee? Too groggy and disoriented to figure out how to respond, she went into autopilot, got dressed, and stumbled out to the coffee station.

Returning to the room, Adelle found Barbara dressed in the same sloppy sweatshirt and jeans as the previous day. And fuzzy pink socks.

At least she changed her socks.

Once again, Barbara was propped up on her bed, hunched over her laptop. Adelle set the coffee down on the bedside table. Barbara muttered, "Thanks," but didn't bother to look up. *This girl is a real piece of work*, Adelle thought. *No, that's not what a professional host should be thinking.*

Adelle swallowed hard and tried a different approach. "See you at breakfast," she said, forcing a smile into her voice. "We're meeting in …" Adelle paused and looked at her watch. *For goodness' sake. What is she doing up so early?* "an hour and ten minutes."

"Roger," Barbara confirmed.

Debbie and Tilly surely didn't dress alike, Adelle observed, as they walked through the dining room entranceway. Debbie wore white slacks and a bright pink sweater with a patterned scarf thrown stylishly over her shoulder. Tilly was wearing khaki slacks and a light blue, long-sleeved cotton shirt. *And hiking boots? Who wore hiking boots on a cruise?* Adelle tried not to stare.

"I see you've noticed Tilly's fashionable choice of footwear," Debbie said, taking her place at the table.

"There's nothing wrong with them," Tilly huffed. "The brochure said to wear sturdy shoes." She wagged her finger at Debbie's bright pink sandals. "We'll see who gets the last laugh when you end up on your butt."

Tilly waved to an older couple walking by their table.

"He's not well," Tilly said, lowering her voice. "She's concerned that he is going to overdo it."

"Tilly," Debbie smirked, "Were you rubbernecking again?"

"Maybe a little," Tilly admitted. "You should try it instead of blabbering all the time. You might learn something. Besides, it wasn't my fault. They were sitting near me when I was quilting on the deck. They should have talked quieter."

Barbara took her phone out of her pocket and stated typing. *How rude*, Adelle thought. It looked like the real Barbara was back. There was an awkward silence as the other women stared at the oblivious Barbara.

"Tilly, are you a quilter?" Adelle asked, changing the topic.

"Let's just say she fidgets," Debbie said.

Tilly turned and high-fived Debbie. "Good one!"

Fascinated, Adelle listened to their local guide as he conducted their morning motor coach tour of Budapest. Generations of his family had lived in Budapest and he was proud to share his city with guests. Adelle was surprised to learn that Budapest had been two cities, Buda and Pest, until they merged in 1873. Their tour started on the more modern east bank, Pest.

"This avenue reminds me of the Champs-Élysées in Paris," Teresa whispered as they drove along the wide Andrassy Avenue. "Look at those shops and theaters. They remind me of Broadway in New York." When the guide pointed out the National Opera House, Teresa sat up excitedly. "Neo-Renaissance," she said.

"Look at that porch with the veranda on top," Adelle heard Tilly say behind them.

"The correct terms are portico and loggia," Teresa quietly informed Adelle.

At the end of the Avenue, they parked at the gateway to the City Park area, continuing their tour on foot. In Hero's Square, Adelle looked up in awe at the huge sculptures. The seven fierce warriors on horseback represented the tribal leaders who had brought the Magyar people to Hungary in 896. There were also more than a dozen large statues of other distinguished men from Hungary's history. Adelle was grateful to have time to read each of the explanatory plaques.

When the group reconvened, the guide suggested that some passengers might want to come back later and explore the City Park area during their afternoon free time. It was home to a spectacular castle and thermal baths, including different mineral pools that were built in 1881.

The group re-boarded their motor coach and drove past more historical buildings, including the large and beautiful St. Stephen's Basilica and the famous Budapest Parliament Building, inspired by the Palace of Westminster in London.

That's why it seemed familiar, Adelle realized.

Many of the other monuments and buildings in Budapest had also been built in 1896, as part of their millennial celebrations.

Millennial? They had a thousand-year celebration over one hundred and twenty years ago? Up until now, Adelle thought a hundred-year celebration was noteworthy.

They drove past Café Gerbeaud, a traditional coffeehouse that had opened in 1870. Their guide described the interior, decorated in marble and exotic wood, rococo-style ceilings, and ornate chandeliers.

No drive-through window here.

The motor coach crossed the Danube and parked at Buda Castle at the top of the steep hill. The castle had been built in the fourteenth century, but had been heavily damaged in World War II, when its secret tunnels had served as a hospital. The tunnels were then converted into bomb shelters in the not-so-distant Soviet era.

Their guide led them along the cobbled streets. Tilly was right. Stable footwear was a must for these cobblestones. Adelle wondered if Debbie had taken her sister's advice to change her shoes. Fashionable sandals definitely wouldn't work here.

They made their way through the various small squares to Fisherman's Bastion. The lookout towers were built in the nineteenth century with the seven turrets representing the seven founding tribes of Hungary. Adelle recognized the fortification as the one she had seen from the ship the previous night. It was even more whimsical in the daylight. And the view! She stood back as the eager amateur photographers jostled for the best angle of Pest across the Danube.

"It's safer back here," she heard an amused female voice observe. Turning, she saw another woman who had stepped aside.

"Hi, I'm Eileen," she said. "We're on the same bus. Thankfully, cameras are digital now or Bill would be out of film already."

"Bill?"

Eileen pointed out her husband leaning on the short wall, swiveling from side to side as he took pictures of the panoramic view.

Their guide waited patiently for everyone to take their pictures. Then he led the group through the city's old streets and around several medieval buildings.

"This," the guide proudly said, "is our eight-hundred-year-old Matthias Church."

The church was breathtaking. Adelle and Eileen admired the colorful tiled roof and delicate turrets, while Bill took photos from every conceivable angle.

The group scattered, and Adelle found herself at the Presidential Palace in time for the hourly changing of the guard. It was a short ceremony with spectacular choreography including twirling rifles, salutes, and a drum corp. She noticed the couple Tilly had gossiped about at breakfast. Was that Barbara standing behind them? Talking on her phone? She was missing the pageantry!

Dinner was another amazing feast. For an appetizer, Tilly ordered the meaty Hungarian farmer's plate, Debbie the pear salad, Teresa the poached scallops, and Adelle selected the roasted eggplant and garlic soup. Barbara passed on the appetizers. *No wonder she's so skinny.*

Adelle was pleased that the women had gathered to eat dinner together. It was fun to hear about each of their adventures, even though Barbara had "nothing to report." Teresa had gone back to the Opera House with new Australian friends. Adelle admired how she seemed so confident and relaxed, approaching other passengers with ease. The sisters had returned to the thermal baths. When Adelle asked to hear more, Debbie and Tilly started to giggle.

"It's your fault." Debbie chuckled and jabbed her finger at Tilly.

"No, it's not," Tilly said, jabbing her back. "The pamphlet wasn't very clear."

"The English one probably was, but you insisted on picking up the Hungarian one."

"Good exercise for the brain," huffed Tilly.

Debbie described their visit. They had paid the entrance fee, received wristbands, changed into their bathing suits, and soaked in each of the various mineral pools.

"Tell them about the chess players," Tilly said.

"Yes, the chess players …" Debbie's eyes twinkled as she described how surprised they were to see a group of older men sitting in one of the pools, playing chess.

"When it was time to leave," Debbie continued, "we went to find towels. Towels were not supplied." She looked at Tilly. "Apparently, we were supposed to bring our own towels."

"The hand blowers worked just fine," Tilly said.

"We looked ridiculous, but not as ridiculous as we looked when we tried to exit."

The sisters burst out laughing again.

"What happened?" asked Teresa.

"We couldn't figure out how to make the exit turnstile work," Debbie replied.

Chuckling, the sisters described how they finally dropped to their hands and knees and crawled out under the turnstile.

Adelle hoped there was lots of room. Tilly was petite, but Debbie was full-figured, to put it politely.

When they stood up and brushed themselves off, they heard snickering and a smattering of applause behind them. They turned around to see several of the chess players lined up at the exit. The first one in line grinned broadly and bowed gallantly. Then he unfastened his wristband, inserted it into a little slot on the turnstile, pushed, and strutted out. He bowed again, doffing his cap as he passed. Following his lead, each of the remaining chess players repeated the ceremonious exit.

"What did you do then?" Adelle asked, wiping tears of laughter from her eyes.

"At first, we were mortified," Debbie said.

"I'm still mortified," Tilly added, winking at Adelle. "Debbie curtsied. I curtsied. And then we walked in the opposite direction of the men."

Debbie grinned. "Another Tilly classic!"

After dinner, the women joined the other passengers on the top deck as they sailed out of Budapest. Adelle was mesmerized by the golden lights dancing on the river as they slid past the ancient floodlit buildings and monuments. On the left bank, she recognized Buda Castle before they sailed under the iconic Chain Bridge. Its cable lines looked like strings of pearls with its hundreds of lit bulbs hanging between the two support pillars. Adelle recognized the beautiful Matthias Church and the seven pointy towers of Fisherman's Bastion. She imagined them as sentries stationed over the Danube.

As they sailed past the immense Parliament Building, Adelle recalled that one hundred thousand workers, forty million bricks, and five hundred thousand precious stones were involved in its construction. She was spellbound by the lights, shimmering like diamonds on the Danube.

Adelle turned around for one last glimpse of Budapest, its reflection waving goodbye in the small ripples behind their ship. As the lights faded into the darkness, she bid a fond farewell to the fairytale kingdom of Budapest.

Chapter Two

Danube

Adelle joined Debbie, who was sipping coffee by the railing as their ship sailed toward Vienna.

"Isn't river cruising wonderful?" Debbie gushed. "The swooping birds, the dogs barking on shore, the crisp fall air, the leaves in all their fall colors. The wide-open country sky and sounds remind me of growing up on the farm."

Debbie shared that Tilly was the oldest in the family, followed two years later by twin brothers. Debbie was born ten years after them. "I was an oops," she said brightly. "Maybe that's why I love surprises so much."

Debbie had met her husband when she was in college and they moved to the west coast shortly after graduation. After teaching for several years, she stayed home with their two daughters until they entered high school. Then she started working part-time in a ladies' clothing consignment store. She loved meeting women and helping them recycle their wardrobes. The store eventually came up for sale. "I bought it and have been there ever since," she said happily.

That explains her stylish wardrobe and accessories, Adelle thought. And her obvious love for shopping.

"Who takes care of your business when you're away?" Adelle asked.

"Over the years, I've become close friends with several customers and they help me out from time to time. I've been very fortunate."

The women waved at the passengers from another cruise ship sailing in the opposite direction.

"By the way, thanks again for the Mozart and Strauss concert tickets for tonight," Debbie said.

Adelle had used the onboard credits Maureen had given the group to purchase the last four remaining tickets.

"You're welcome. I'm a bit surprised that Tilly doesn't want to go." *Surprised and disappointed*, Adelle thought. Classical music wasn't her thing, and now she would have to go.

"She's probably looking forward to some quiet time in our room by herself," Debbie said, smiling. "Would you believe she's seventy-two years old?" Debbie asked.

"Really? I thought she was around my age."

"How old are you?" Debbie asked.

"I just turned sixty-two," Adelle replied. *Two years past forced retirement*, she thought ruefully. She had spent the first year saying yes to everyone—volunteer projects, baby-sitting, political campaigns. Retirement was more tiring than working. The second year she had said no to everyone. Except Maureen, she happily realized.

When Tilly had turned sixty-five, the sisters had decided to go on a trip together.

"It's hard to get one-on-one time with Tilly," Debbie explained. "I go home to the farm for a week or two every summer, but the time goes by too quickly. I have my brothers and their wives and my nieces and nephews to visit, and I still stay in touch with old neighbors and friends. Before I know it, it's time to leave and Tilly and I have hardly spent any time together. She tries to get out to the coast each winter for a few days, but she has to split her time with my daughters and their families as well."

The sisters' first trip together had been a week-long bus trip along the east coast. "We had fun, but we promised each other that we would never do a bus trip again," Debbie said.

"Why not?" asked Adelle.

"We were in a different hotel every night. Early each morning we had to get up, pack, rush through breakfast, and board our bus on time. And if you haven't noticed, we're pretty different from each other. Tilly's an early bird and I'm a night owl. She needs quiet time and her own space and I like being with other people. She likes her routines and I need variety."

Debbie rolled her eyes. "And then, there was George …"

"Who was George?"

"He was the most annoying person we have ever met. Picture yourself on a bus for seven days with a man who talked all the time. And I do mean all the time."

Adelle coughed into the crook of her elbow, hiding her smile. She was having no trouble picturing George.

Debbie barely took a breath and continued.

"He insisted on sitting in the front seat. He read every sign … out loud! Speed limits, billboards, signs advertising the 'best fish and chips in the world.'" Debbie chuckled. "Have you ever noticed how many restaurants claim to make the 'best fish and chips in the world?'"

Adelle laughed. Debbie was right!

"A few years later, Tilly's husband and I convinced her to travel with me again. Since she had planned the disastrous bus trip, it was my turn to pick our vacation. We went to Ireland for ten days." Debbie giggled. "Do yourself a favor and don't bring it up with Tilly."

"What happened?" Adelle asked. How could a trip to Ireland possibly go wrong?

Debbie had booked only the first and last night's accommodation.

"It was great for me. We rented a car and drove from place to place in a generally clockwise direction. There was no bus to catch, no schedule. We could get up whenever we wanted."

Sounds good to me, Adelle thought. "Tilly didn't like that?"

"She hated it." Debbie explained that Tilly got more and more stressed each day. She needed an itinerary, and to know in advance where they were going to stay each night.

"Tilly thought it would be good for our brains to navigate the old-fashioned way, with maps, so we declined the GPS car rental option." Debbie frowned. "She detests technology. She used to drive the farm machinery before they got all fancy. Now everything is computerized and she can't help in the field anymore."

Adelle thought of her husband and how frustrated he would be if that happened to him. After doing accounting in his home office all winter, he loved when spring came and he could help his best friend put the crops in. Now he was in his glory, helping with harvest. Adelle felt sorry for Tilly.

Adelle thought of another difficulty. "Don't they drive on the other side of the road in Ireland?" she asked.

"They do," Debbie replied. "But that wasn't the hardest part."

"It wasn't?" Adelle couldn't imagine driving on the left side of the road.

Debbie rolled her eyes. "We booked a standard."

"Let me guess," Adelle said. "It's better for the brain."

Debbie laughed. "You're catching on!"

"How did you decide where to go each day?"

"We stayed at bed-and-breakfasts," Debbie replied. "Sometimes I asked the other guests where they had been and what they had enjoyed. Other times I would stop at a town or village and look for a postcard stand."

Adelle was puzzled.

"Local postcards always feature nearby attractions. We found a charming castle that way. With Tilly as navigator though, I needed help with the road signs. Let's just say I started calling her George."

Debbie chuckled. "My poor sister. The only part of the trip she looked forward to was finding a pub at the end of the day so she could self-medicate."

"Good for the brain," Adelle said. They both laughed.

"Speaking of George, here she comes now." Debbie smiled and waved at her sister.

"Here you are," Tilly said. "Gabbing again. We're going to be late for the German lesson, and you promised to go with me." She winked at Adelle, hooked arms with Debbie, and led her away.

Adelle decided to burn off some calories on the walking track. Halfway around, she passed Teresa, who was deep in conversation with a man between the track and the railing. As she walked by, she overheard Teresa say, "I'm tired of kindergarten."

That's odd. Adelle would have never guessed that Teresa was a kindergarten teacher, although her perfect posture and direct approach radiated authority.

Adelle walked another lap.

Am I rubbernecking? Maybe.

This time she heard Teresa say, "I need a man."

Next lap around, they were gone.

Adelle met the mystery man—and his wife—when she went down for lunch. They were the Australian couple Teresa had met the previous day in Budapest. Teresa introduced Adelle to Rod and his wife Vicki, and invited her to join them for lunch. Adelle sat down, determined to find out more about the Australians. And Teresa.

"Is this your first river cruise?" she asked Rod and Vicki.

It was their third river cruise. Rod was a history buff interested in UNESCO World Heritage Sites, and this trip featured a lot of them.

"What does UNESCO stand for?" Adelle asked.

"United Nations Educational, Scientific, and Cultural Organization," Rod replied. "We live close to a site in

Melbourne. Carlton Gardens and the Royal Exhibition Building." He turned to address Teresa directly. "It's one of the world's last exhibition buildings from the nineteenth century."

As Rod described UNESCO's mandate and criteria, Adelle noticed Teresa paying rapt attention. Either she was really interested in UNESCO or she was really interested in Rod. Adelle hoped it was the former.

Teresa glanced at Adelle. "Rod and I have been discussing the architectural features of Budapest." She turned back to Rod as he went into more depth about eclectic building styles.

Vicki nudged Adelle. "Let's go and get our soup."

"Good idea," Adelle said gratefully. She had heard enough about architecture in the last two days.

As they made their way to the buffet, Adelle thanked Vicki.

"No worries mate," Vicki said. "I've heard it all before. Too many times to count."

"Building details aren't my cup of tea," Adelle admitted. "What are you looking forward to on this trip?" To Adelle's chagrin, Vicki went on and on about tapestries. In great detail.

After lunch, Adelle attended the presentation on Viennese coffeehouses. Scanning the lounge, she noticed two men sitting together.

"May I join you?" Adelle asked, just as Lee was about to start.

"Please do."

The presentation was very informative. They learned that people in Vienna had been flocking to coffeehouses for over three centuries. The experience was an important aspect of their culture. Lee taught them how to order the many variations of coffee. Best of all, after the presentation, they sampled delicious coffee and tortes.

"I found it interesting that some of the coffeehouses feature stringed quartets," the man sitting beside Adelle said.

Adelle had a sudden idea. Maybe she could light two candles with one match.

"Do you like classical music?"

Chapter Three

Vienna

"Good morning," Debbie smiled brightly as she greeted Adelle at breakfast. "You missed a great concert last night. You should have seen the costumes the entertainers were wearing!"

Adelle smiled and nodded while Debbie shared her many observations. Then she turned to Teresa. "How was your date?"

The other four women stared at her with blank faces.

Oops, did I say that out loud?

Debbie and Teresa burst out laughing. Even Barbara had a hint of a smile on her face.

"He was okay until he started snoring," Debbie said. "At intermission, all he did was talk on and on about his partner."

"His business partner?" All eyes turned to Adelle again.

Uh-oh. Adelle's stomach started to flutter.

"His life partner," Teresa replied, emphasizing the word life.

Adelle berated herself for being so naïve. How could she have been so mistaken? She replayed her conversation with the men in her mind. Oh … when one of them said they were into specialty coffee, she had assumed he meant they were partners in a coffee business.

Time to change the topic.

"Barbara, what did you think of the evening?"

Barbara proceeded to lecture them on the connection between people who enjoyed classical music and their mathematical acumen.

"Hogwash," Tilly said, crossing her arms. "I'm good with numbers, but I would rather listen to country music any time. You can learn a lot about people from well-written lyrics."

Barbara ignored Tilly and resumed her lecture. Using terms that Adelle had never heard before, Barbara explained the correlation between classical music enthusiasts and people with above-average intelligence.

"That's why I listen to Mozart instead of country music," Barbara said, smiling smugly at Tilly.

Adelle couldn't think of any more topics.

Adelle loved the drive along the Ringstrasse, the gracious boulevard circling the old city center of Vienna. Built in 1857 to replace the thirteenth century walls, the boulevard was lined with grand buildings, monuments, and parks in addition to the showy mansions and palaces the wealthy and nobility had built, trying to outdo each other.

"Keeping up with the Joneses," Adelle heard from the motor coach seat behind her.

"Shush, Tilly," whispered Debbie. "Everyone can hear you."

"No, they can't," Tilly replied.

As they passed the world-famous Opera House, Adelle blushed as she recalled her match-making blunder. Soon she was distracted by the Austrian Parliament building. It looked more like a Greek-Roman temple than the heart of political activity.

The walking tour started in front of the buildings and courtyards of the Hofburg Imperial Palace, which had been built in the thirteenth century. It had since been expanded several times, and served as the winter residence of the powerful Habsburg dynasty.

Tilly seemed fascinated with the Spanish Riding School, the home of the Lipizzaner stallions. Their tour group was fortunate to get a glimpse of two huge prancing stallions as their trainers led them from their stalls to the training area. Adelle was surprised to learn that the foals were black at birth, then turned lighter as they grew older.

"Just like us," Tilly said.

They continued on to the old city center, a maze of medieval streets. Adelle recalled how eager Rod was to check the historic center of Vienna off his list of UNESCO sites.

Their local guide led them to St. Stephen's Cathedral, and pointed out its colorful roof and high tower. "You can see the cathedral from almost anywhere in the city," she said. "If you get lost, just look up. You will likely see the tower and then you can find your way back."

"Look at all the fashion boutiques," Debbie cried, pointing out the shops as they walked further on.

"Shush. I can't hear the guide," Tilly complained, winking at Adelle.

When the tour dispersed for personal time, the sisters and Adelle treated themselves in a nearby coffeehouse. Tilly shared what she knew about the Habsburgs.

"Tilly loves to read," Debbie interjected. "Just don't expect her to hear what you're saying when she has her nose buried in a book. The ceiling could fall in and she would never know it."

"She's right," agreed Tilly. "I really like historical fiction. The history comes alive and it's an interesting way to learn."

Tilly told them how the Habsburgs had ruled countries in Europe for hundreds of years. She seemed to know a lot about Maria Theresa Habsburg, the only female ruler of the Habsburg Empire. "Did you know that Marie Antoinette was the youngest of her fifteen children? She was married off at age fourteen to strengthen the alliance between Austria and France."

Adelle tried to imagine the pressure the young teenager must have felt. How could she possibly keep two countries happy?

Adelle was exhausted at dinner that night. She had spent the afternoon traipsing from boutique to boutique until Debbie finally took pity on her and suggested Adelle sit and have coffee while she continued browsing. Adelle was grateful to get back to the ship.

Debbie got more and more excited as she described the emerging fashion trends in Europe. As soon as she stopped to take a drink, Adelle asked Tilly and Teresa about their afternoon excursion to the market with the ship's chef.

"The market was interesting," Teresa said. She turned to Debbie with a glint in her eye. "Tilly picked up every fruit and vegetable in sight."

Debbie laughed. "I guess it runs in the family."

"The chef knew most of the stall vendors," Tilly said, "and we got to sample some Austrian cheeses and baklava."

"What's baklava?" Barbara asked, briefly taking her eyes off her phone.

"It's a sweet pastry filled with nuts and honey. It's on tonight's menu. You'll have to try it," Tilly said. She raised one eyebrow when Barbara looked down again. "After the chef answered all our questions, he continued to pick out provisions for the ship."

"When he was done," Teresa continued, "he gave us the choice to take the subway back with him or spend time on our own."

"That's when Teresa saved the day," Tilly said, looking directly at Adelle.

Uh-oh. Maybe Adelle's idea hadn't been so great after all. Adelle had arranged the market excursion through Lee, hoping to make up for her faux pas with Teresa's date. She knew Tilly liked gardening, and the way Teresa always raved about their delicious meals, Adelle assumed she liked cooking. Although shopping wasn't Adelle's thing, she purposely went with Debbie to split up the group and give the sisters a break from each other.

"Tilly told me that she would have to return to Vienna some other time," Teresa said. "She really wanted to tour the Schönbrunn Palace."

"It was the summer home of the Habsburgs," Tilly explained.

"It's one of the UNESCO sites," Teresa added. "It was built to compete with the Palace of Versailles near Paris."

The chef had shown Teresa and Tilly how to take the subway to the palace. They raved about the imperial apartments, the lavishly decorated rooms, and the formal gardens.

"We learned a bit about the reign of Maria Theresa Habsburg," Teresa continued. "She introduced many military and bureaucratic reforms, as well as initiatives in public health."

"All in all, it was a very interesting day," Tilly said, smiling. Suddenly she frowned and looked at Barbara. "We saw you there. Trailing behind the coffee partners."

"No, you didn't," Barbara curtly replied.

Before Tilly could argue, Adelle quickly asked Debbie to describe some of the boutiques they had visited.

Eventually, Tilly held up her hand to get Debbie to stop talking. "Here comes the baklava." She pointed to their server, carefully balancing five dessert plates.

"As Marie Antoinette said, let them eat cake."

Chapter Four

Melk

The dancers swirled around the ballroom, full skirts billowing, tuxedo tails sailing, as the faint strains of the "Blue Danube Waltz" played in the background. Adelle smiled down on the room as she floated above. Naked.

Click.

Startled out of her sleep, Adelle sat up. *Ballroom dancers?* She opened her eyes and saw nothing. It was pitch black. She lay back down, gripping her blankets under her chin. "Barbara?"

Silence. Adelle realized that she probably woke up when the door clicked as Barbara was leaving their cabin.

Naked?

Maybe her dream was due to the magazine article she had read about dreams and their interpretations. Didn't the article state that dreaming about being naked in public was a sign of feeling ashamed? After all, she had made the mistake of arranging the trip for Tilly and Teresa with the chef. If Teresa hadn't acted on Tilly's disappointment, they would have missed touring Schönbrunn Palace.

There was another possibility. Naked could symbolize that in her heart of hearts, she didn't have the foggiest idea what she was doing as a tour host.

Adelle sighed. *Better shape up or ship out.* She smiled. *Good one.*

Adelle and Debbie stood at the railing on the top deck, taking in the beautiful view as they sailed up the Wachau Valley between Krems and Melk.

"The Danube looks more like pewter than blue," Debbie observed. "See how the river and the overcast sky make the colors of the leaves pop? This is a photographer's dream."

Adelle agreed. The deep yellow, burnt orange, and red leaves were stunning. As were the quaint villages with their orange-tiled roofs and the golden vineyard terraces built into the steep hillsides. Crumbling gray castles towered over the valley.

Lee started his commentary over the top-deck speakers.

"Coming up, you will see the small town of Durnstein. This is where Richard the Lionheart of England was held captive by Duke Leopold the Fifth. Richard was called Lionheart because of his reputation as a great military leader and warrior. But I'll bet you didn't know that he was also known in the Occitan dialect as 'Oc-e-Non,' which literally means yes and no. He was a man of few words."

Like Barbara, thought Adelle, half-listening to the rest of Lee's commentary. Barbara was so secretive. She joined the group for breakfast and dinner, but most of the time she just sat there silently and fiddled with her phone. She rarely joined in the conversation. The women were starting to talk about her. Nothing too dramatic, just remarks here and there.

Adelle straightened her shoulders. Maureen was counting on her. She would do her professional best to make everyone happy, including Barbara. Or perhaps in spite of her.

After lunch, the ship docked in Melk and the passengers rode the motor coaches up to the Benedictine Abbey, perched on the hilltop overlooking the village. After they passed through the high-arched entrance into the large courtyard, their guide asked them to please be quiet and respectful. There were monks and nine hundred students working and studying there.

The first monks had found their way to Melk in 1089. They had set up a monastery in the old castle, which was given to them by Count Leopold II. The Abbey had been rebuilt during the eighteenth century, after the original palace was destroyed by fire. It was an enormous palace, with ceremonial courts, grand halls, and guest apartments. The opulent dining room, Marble Hall, had been decorated by world-class artists and sculptors, and was renowned for its gilt frescoes. Its painted ceiling was said to rival the Sistine Chapel.

The monastic library had soon become well-known for its extensive manuscript collection. Their tour group walked through the dark two-story room with floor-to-ceiling bookshelves containing eighty thousand leather-bound medieval manuscripts, many of which were handwritten. Adelle half expected to see a robed monk hunched over a small desk, dipping his quill into ink as he copied a manuscript by hand.

"What was your favorite part of the tour?" Adelle asked Teresa as they walked down the cobblestone street through the village of Melk on their way back to the ship.

"The marble spiral staircase from the library exit down to the church. At first I thought it went forever, and then I realized it was an illusion. There were mirrors at the top and the bottom. Very clever."

As they strolled along, Teresa went on and on about the fresco ceiling and the fluting and the gilded pillars of the baroque church. Adelle noticed Debbie and Tilly waving at them from a café window. "Look," Adelle said, relieved. "Let's join them for coffee."

"Goose gut," Tilly said, greeting them with a wide smile.

Debbie started to laugh. "No, sis. It's Grüss Gott, silly!" She explained to Adelle and Teresa that the phrase meant hello in Austrian.

"Close enough," Tilly said. "Thirty, thirty-first, same thing only different."

"What?" asked Adelle. Had she missed something?

The sisters laughed. Their rural community had been settled by European families in the late 1800s and early to mid 1900s. Several expressions had survived through the generations. One of their neighbors, when told by her son that there was no September thirty-first, had indignantly replied, "thirty, thirty-first, same thing only different."

"She had a point," Teresa said.

"As our grandmother was fond of saying," countered Tilly, "'the poor dear was just wrong, and she should be pitied.'"

Adelle shifted the topic to Maria Theresa Habsburg. Teresa and Tilly both liked her. "Did you hear the guide say that in her lifetime, Maria Theresa often visited the Abbey and that there had been ghost sightings there ever since?"

"Speaking of ghosts," Debbie said, pointing across the street, "isn't that Barbara walking behind Rod and Vicki?"

"Look at that fool," Tilly said. "It's like her phone is another limb. She needs to watch where she's going."

Adelle scrambled to change the topic back to safer common ground. "Teresa, what do you like about Maria?"

"The more I learn about her, the more inspired I am." Teresa stirred her coffee. "Did you know she governed for forty years, most of that time as a widow?"

"With fifteen children," Tilly huffed. "She should have put her family first and stayed home with her kids."

Teresa put her spoon down. "She was working to provide a better future for her family and for her people," she said evenly. "Education and medicine mattered to her. She was credited with many advances in her day."

Tilly crossed her arms. "If she had stayed at home and taken better care of her family, her youngest daughter wouldn't have been married off to that French prince and she wouldn't have lost her head."

"Look, it's starting to rain," Adelle said, pointing out the window. "We better get back to the ship before we get soaked."

Tilly brushed by Teresa on her way out the door. "Poor dear," she muttered.

Chapter Five

Passau

The next morning, Adelle bumped into Lee as she walked past the ship's reception area. "Thanks for your commentary yesterday," she said. "I especially liked the story of Richard the Lionheart."

"You're welcome," he said, smiling. "Sometimes I'm afraid that people might see this as an ABC tour, so I try to add some people stories each time."

"ABC tour?" Adelle asked.

"Another bloody castle," he said, laughing. "By the way, while I've got you here, I want to give you a heads up. When we're in Passau today, make sure you and your group take note of the high-water marks drawn on some of the buildings. We might have a small problem brewing." A crew member tugged on Lee's arm and told him the captain wanted to see him. "I'll check in with you later," he said as he rushed off.

At the mention of brewing, Adelle craved her morning coffee. She saw Tilly standing at the coffee station. "You're up early."

"I'm up early every morning," Tilly said. "The night owl likes to sleep in."

Adelle smiled as she recalled the previous evening. She suspected Teresa would be sleeping late as well. Barbara had been working on her laptop after dinner, so Adelle had decided to visit the lounge. She was pleased to find Debbie and Teresa sitting with a group including Eileen and Bill. She learned that Bill was a physiotherapist, vacationing with other classmates and their spouses to celebrate their thirty-year class reunion. It had been a fun but late night.

Adelle noticed the tote bag Tilly was carrying. "Is that your quilting project?" she asked.

"I make fidget quilts," Tilly said, pulling a small quilt out of the bag. It was lap-sized and very colorful. Each small block featured different textures. Adelle saw pieces with short zippers, large buttons, yarn tassels, a denim jean pocket, and Velcro strips. "The idea is to exercise the fingers and hands," Tilly said, demonstrating. "These are useful for people with dementia. Often they have restless hands and it gives them something to do."

Restless hands. Adelle bet Teresa's kindergarten students would love fidget quilts. Common interests always brought people together.

Their local guide explained that Passau was known as the City of Three Rivers. He pointed out where the Ilz River from the north and the Inn River from the south joined the Danube. Adelle looked up at the high-water marks that had been drawn on a nearby building. They were higher than her. Poor Passau, she thought. It must have been terrifying when the waters poured in.

"Don't worry," the guide said, answering a question. "We've had some rain in the last few days and the rivers are high, but nothing like they were in June of 2013. That was the worst flooding we've experienced in five hundred years." He continued leading them through the narrow streets of Old Town, past colorful buildings and traditional patrician homes. "Thankfully, our famous St. Stephen's Cathedral wasn't damaged. Wait until you hear the pipe organ."

Adelle followed their guide into the cathedral. She noticed another group from their ship in the pews up near the front. Was that Barbara slouched behind the physios? Adelle looked again. No, this woman had black hair. Besides, Barbara was in Salzburg for the day. Adelle settled in to listen to the music.

Teresa and the sisters were standing together outside the cathedral as Adelle's group filed out.

"Did you hear that pipe organ?" Debbie asked Adelle. "Wasn't it magnificent?"

"It has seventeen thousand, nine hundred seventy-four pipes," Tilly said.

"Or there about," teased Debbie.

"What amazed me," said Teresa, "is how the organist can play all five parts from the main keyboard, either one at a time or all together."

"And the acoustics were incredible," gushed Debbie.

Teresa agreed. "Not bad for a cathedral that was built in 1688."

Debbie's eyes twinkled. "Wait until I tell the rest of the family that 'surround sound' has been around for over three hundred years!"

Before the pre-dinner briefing, Adelle was tempted to check her emails. Then she stopped herself, remembering one of her favorite sayings. *Temptations are a reminder that I have a choice.* She chose to respect the deal she had made with her granddaughter. Adelle smiled, recalling their conversation at the airport.

Adelle's granddaughter had asked her to support her class in the school technology challenge. "Grandma, you can help us win," she had said. "All you have to do is show proof of reduced screen time for the next two weeks." The idea made sense to Adelle. She wasn't worried about her husband, Wes. When he was farming, he was farming. He hadn't even taken his cell phone with him.

Adelle could still see the smile on her granddaughter's face when she hugged her goodbye and handed over her phone for safekeeping.

Dinner was strained. Barbara replied "nothing to report" when Adelle asked her about her trip to Salzburg. She kept her head down, typing on her phone the whole meal. Tilly seemed grumpy and didn't say a word. Teresa wasn't there; she was eating with the physio group. Debbie seemed oblivious to the tension around the table and chatted away as always.

Adelle was puzzled until she met up with Debbie in the lounge later. Apparently, Tilly had been highly offended by something Teresa had said earlier. Instead of showing interest in the fidget quilt, Teresa had peppered Tilly with questions about dementia and what she was looking for in a senior's home. Tilly was furious. She said she wasn't anywhere near ready to be put out to pasture. Debbie told Adelle not to worry, Tilly would get over it. Adelle hoped so.

To make matters worse, Lee had nabbed Adelle on her way back to her room. He had bad news. The river was swollen from all the rain upstream, and they might not fit under an upcoming bridge. There was a good chance they might have to continue by motor coach.

Chapter Six

Regensburg

None of the women showed up for breakfast. Adelle sat by herself, growing more and more anxious. Had the sisters heard about the looming motor coach trip? Were they sulking in their room? And where was Teresa? Was she avoiding everyone because of Tilly? *Or chasing another married man?* Eileen had casually mentioned that one of the physio's husbands and Teresa were spending a lot of time together.

Barbara wasn't at breakfast, either. After Adelle had awakened briefly to the tune of the annoying "Blue Danube Waltz" playing in her brain, she had gone back to sleep. When she woke again, Barbara was gone. She was probably ticked off that Adelle hadn't provided barista coffee service.

Adelle stirred her coffee, worried that all of her group had given up on her. She felt like a container of sour cream in the back of her fridge—forgotten and past its best-before date. She was letting Maureen down.

Don't be ridiculous, she scolded herself as she left the restaurant and headed up to the light breakfast station on the deck. *This is what happens when you don't get enough sleep. You always imagine the worst-case scenario.* There was probably a good reason why her friends weren't there.

Then she spotted them eating breakfast together on the deck. Laughing. Even Barbara was there. Laughing.

Feeling the sting of rejection, Adelle spun around and fled down the blurring stairs.

The young woman at the ship's registration desk hadn't asked any questions when Adelle switched to the "easy" walking group for the morning tour. She kept her head down, searching for an available seat on the motor coach.

"Hi, Adelle," she heard a familiar voice call out. "Come sit with us back here."

Adelle looked up long enough to see Eileen waving. She wiped her tears away, forced a smile, and headed to the back of the coach. "Don't mind me," she said. "My allergies are acting up this morning."

Eileen and Bill were good company as their group strolled through the cobbled streets and colorful houses of Regensburg. Another UNESCO site, it was the oldest city on the Danube, and one of the best-preserved medieval towns in Europe. Its history dated back nearly two thousand years. Bill told Adelle that he preferred the "easy" walking tour. The leisurely pace gave him more time to compose better photos.

As they walked with their guide, Adelle thought of the women. Tilly would note that there were 984 listed buildings in Old Town. Teresa would love the gothic St. Peter's Cathedral with its twin renaissance spires. Adelle smiled, thinking of Debbie when she heard that Regensburg had the highest concentration of bars in Germany. That girl loved to party!

Their tour guide pointed out Roman gates that were built in 179 AD. Fortunately, the city center had escaped damage in the war, and its architectural treasures and half-timbered buildings were still standing. Most were still inhabited by shops and families.

As they walked along the old stone bridge, built in the twelfth century, Adelle was amazed to see traffic still driving on it. Next to the bridge was the old town hall, which was now home to a museum and tourist office. Seeing the postcard displays, Adelle remembered Debbie's story of using postcards to plan their day's itinerary. That reminded her of the looming bus tour disaster.

"Allergies bothering you again?" Eileen gently asked.

Adelle nodded. She felt badly about fibbing, but she was too ashamed to admit her failures and fears. Her greatest joy was making new friends, but her greatest fear was letting them down. Eileen looked at her for a moment and then suggested Adelle join her and Bill for lunch at the Historic Sausage Kitchen, Germany's oldest restaurant.

The finger-sized sausages grilled over beech wood and served with sauerkraut and sweet grainy mustard were delicious. Adelle could hardly believe that the small kitchen and dining room had been in the same spot since 1135. Cheered up by the food and the company, Adelle headed back to the ship.

Eileen had saved a seat for Adelle at the pre-dinner briefing in the lounge. As she took her place, she heard snickers, chuckles, and some outright belly laughs. Adelle was sure she heard Tilly's voice near the back, saying, "they look ridiculous." She smiled as she recognized Debbie's voice, shushing her sister.

Adelle looked up. Lee and the concierge, Nikola, were walking into the room dressed in lederhosen, the traditional leather German shorts and suspenders. Tilly was right. They looked ridiculous. The men had obviously swapped breeches. Burly Nikola was stuffed into skintight lederhosen, threatening to burst. Lee was swimming in oversized lederhosen. Adelle joined the boisterous laughing and clapping. She hadn't laughed that hard in a long time.

Lee smiled, waved, and then bowed repeatedly to the crowd. "Good evening," he began, grinning widely. "How do you like our lederhosen?" He and Nikola strutted a few steps, turning and posing like models on a runway, as the crowd clapped enthusiastically.

Lee raised his hand and waited for everyone to settle down. "I have some good news and some bad news. I'll begin with the bad news … but remember, it's followed by good news." He paused making sure he had everyone's full attention. "As you may have noticed in Passau, this area is prone to flooding when there is too much rain upstream. Unfortunately, there has been just enough rain that we won't fit under the next bridge."

Oh no! Disaster confirmed. Adelle's heart began to race.

Lee quickly raised his arms to stop the crescendo of groans around the room. "Now for the good news." He grinned and paused for effect. "Instead of continuing our trip by motor coach, we will simply swap ships."

Swap ships?

Lee smiled reassuringly. "One of our sister ships, sailing in the reverse direction from Amsterdam to Budapest, is on the other side of the impassable bridge." He let that information sink in. "We'll simply exchange places with its passengers. You will hardly know the difference. Our crew will stay onboard this ship. Except for Nikola and me. We will join you on your new ship."

There was a smattering of applause. Lee bowed in acknowledgement and the clapping increased. No one clapped louder than Adelle.

"Good save," Adelle murmured to Lee as she passed him on her way to dinner. The dreaded bus tour had been avoided. That would make Tilly and Debbie very happy. And Adelle was happy that once again, the cruise line was well prepared and had taken care of all the details.

Adelle wished she could join Debbie, Tilly, Teresa, and Barbara for dinner, but it was too late. She had already accepted Eileen's invitation to eat with the physios. She would connect with the women later.

Chapter Seven

Nuremburg

The next morning, Adelle mumbled her apologies as she hurried down the aisle of the motor coach.

"Sit here," Eileen said, patting the seat beside her. "Running late?"

Nodding, Adelle tried to catch her breath. She was indeed running late. When she had crept in from the lengthy dinner the night before, Barbara was asleep, her bags packed and near the door. Adelle had delayed packing until morning. She was exhausted from the day's emotional roller coaster and hadn't wanted to wake Barbara.

Adelle had slept soundly, stirring briefly when Barbara left and then she must have drifted back to sleep. A sharp knock on the door woke her again. Looking at the time, she panicked. Dressing quickly, she threw her things into her carry-on and rushed to catch the motor coach.

Adelle dropped down into her seat. "Where's Bill?" she asked, trying to catch her breath.

Eileen lowered her voice. "He's at the back with Joe, one of his classmates, trying to cheer him up." She pointed to the front of the bus. "His wife, Ann, is sitting up at the front with the annoying video lady."

Sure enough, Ann was sitting with the woman who was constantly videoing, giving a running commentary as she did so. She was always oblivious to everyone around her, talked over the guide, held her iPad high, obstructing the view. When she was also holding an umbrella, she was outright dangerous.

"Joe and Ann have had a bit of a tiff," Eileen explained quietly. Joe's first wife had passed away three years ago and he had remarried since his classmates had last seen him. Everyone found Ann quiet and shy.

"Do you know what the issue is?" Adelle asked. Suddenly, she was worried. Did it have anything to do with Teresa?

"No," Eileen replied, twisting her scarf in her hands. "Breakfast was very awkward for all of us."

Adelle needed to find out what was going on. "Maybe I could join your group for lunch and try and lighten things up?

Eileen brightened immediately. "That would be great!"

During the motor coach tour of the Nuremberg sites, the passengers were quiet as they listened to their guide speak about the Nuremberg trials held in the Palace of Justice. As they drove past Zeppelin Field, Adelle remembered the clips of the massive rallies that she had seen in a documentary. She was surprised how small the field actually was. Sometimes things just weren't what they seemed, she reminded herself.

Their motor coach stopped at the medieval castle perched high over the city. In the Middle Ages, it had been one of the most important imperial castles of the Holy Roman Empire. From the castle, they followed their guide down the cobblestone streets into the old town section. Nuremberg was certainly a city of extremes. It had once been the toy-making capital of Europe.

Adelle caught a whiff of gingerbread, reminding her of baking with her grandmother when she was a girl. Impulsively, she bought gingerbread for each of the women. This was the kind of shopping she enjoyed!

"Hello, stranger," Debbie said brightly, setting her dinner menu aside. "We've missed you."

They missed me!

"You've been avoiding us," Tilly bluntly said.

Adelle's stomach dropped. Is that what they assumed?

"What about you?" Adelle blurted, surprising herself. "Where was everyone at breakfast yesterday?" She felt the pain all over again.

Debbie and Tilly stared at Barbara who was tapping away on her phone. "I emailed you," she said without looking up.

"To tell you we were eating breakfast on the deck, watching the sunrise," Debbie added.

Oh.

Adelle felt foolish. Once again, she had jumped to conclusions. Why hadn't she approached them on the deck instead of assuming they had abandoned her? The last two days of feeling sorry for herself could have been avoided.

She looked up. Everyone was looking at her.

Adelle took a deep breath. She told them about her granddaughter's screen time challenge and why she didn't have her phone with her. Barbara didn't hold back. "A real tour host wouldn't leave her phone at home," she said.

Adelle looked down at her lap. Barbara was right. She picked away at the rest of her dinner in silence.

Chapter Eight

Bamberg

Adelle joined Eileen on the top deck after breakfast, as they sailed from Nuremberg to Bamberg.

"Thanks for your help at lunch yesterday," Eileen said, touching Adelle's arm lightly.

"No problem," Adelle said. When she sat beside Ann at lunch the previous day, Adelle had discreetly discovered what the issue had been between Ann and her husband. The first day onboard, Ann had purposely taken extra time unpacking. It had given her some quiet time and had given Joe the opportunity to catch up with his old friends. When the ship swap had been announced, Joe had teased her about taking forever to pack and unpack. Ann's feelings were hurt. Sharing the incident out loud with Adelle helped her realize that she had overreacted.

"Whatever you said," Eileen said, "it worked. They are nerds in love again."

The friends continued strolling around the track in companionable silence. Adelle reflected on her own experience with overreaction. She wasn't comfortable sharing her conversation with Ann, but knew she could confide in Eileen about the misunderstanding with the women. All that angst over nothing.

"Let it go," Eileen advised kindly when Adelle told her about her struggles the past two days. "They'll probably never know what you went through."

Adelle felt so much better. Except she still didn't know how to interact with Barbara. That morning Adelle had found a short, handwritten note on the bathroom counter:

"Need the room later this morning. Work to do."

Adelle enjoyed the walking tour of Bamberg guided by a student from the local university. He led them through the crooked lanes, pausing to share interesting tidbits of history. Because the railway had never gone through Bamberg and it had failed to attract major industry, the city had not been bombed during World War II. Both sides left Bamberg alone. As a result, it still had its authentic medieval appearance, earning Bamberg UNESCO world heritage status.

Check, thought Adelle. Another site.

Adelle's favorite building was the Old Town Hall. According to legend, the Bishop of Bamberg refused to grant the citizens any land for construction of a town hall. Undeterred, they rammed stakes into the river to create a tiny artificial island. The original building was built on it sometime before 1387. A baroque addition, hanging over the water, was added in the middle of the eighteenth century.

The outside walls were entirely covered with frescoes, painted in such a way that they seemed three dimensional.

Adelle waved at Eileen, standing back as Bill joined the flock of photographers.

"Look at that," Eileen said, laughing as she pointed at the wall. A plaster cherub's leg poked out cheekily from one of the murals.

Later, Adelle joined Debbie and Tilly at a small table outside a busy tavern known for its smoked beer. Debbie was still laughing about the cherub sculpture. "A leg up on history," she quipped.

"Good one, Debbie." Adelle looked around. "How did you order your beer?" She was curious to try the local specialty.

"You need to fight your way through the crowd inside to the back-left corner," Debbie replied. "You talk through a tiny window in the wall."

When Adelle returned with her beer, Tilly told them what she had learned. "They've been serving beer this way since 1405." Tilly swirled her glass. "All beers used to have this smoky taste because the green malt had to be dried over open fires." She grinned at Adelle. "Try it. You'll like it."

Adelle was open to trying anything once. She took a cautious sip.

Yuck! Drinking bitter liquid smoke must be an acquired taste.

"Drink up," Tilly said, chuckling. "It's good for you."

Debbie clinked glasses with her sister. "You and your beer," she said, winking at Adelle.

"She's going to think I'm a souse," Tilly complained.

"Not at all," said Adelle, although she had noticed that Tilly was taking full advantage of the complimentary beer and wine onboard their ship. Tilly wasn't the only one. That morning Adelle had caught Ann reaching under the breakfast station counter to bring out a bottle of champagne. She had explained that a mimosa was a great way to start the day. But only on vacation, she had added, eyes sparkling.

At dinner that night, Adelle noticed how agitated Barbara seemed as she kept stabbing at her phone. She ignored the women, and they ignored her.

Between courses, Teresa raised the topic of senior communities. "Debbie, where do you plan to live in your later years?" she asked.

"To be honest, I haven't given it much thought," Debbie replied. "I guess my plan is to cross that bridge when I get there." She started to giggle. "Or sail under it!"

Teresa chuckled and then asked Adelle the same question. Like Debbie, she hadn't really thought about it. She was still getting used to retirement and Wes was still content to do farm accounting in their home office. He loved to take breaks and putter in their yard. The next phase of their life seemed eons away.

"Tilly, how about you?" Teresa asked.

Tilly thrust out her chin and sat up straight. "I'm going to live in my house on the farm. Forever. They'll have to carry me out."

Adelle sensed Teresa and Tilly gearing up for another argument. "Barbara, what did you learn in Bamberg today?" she asked, desperate to change the topic.

"Nothing," Barbara muttered, not bothering to look up.

Adelle tried again. "I was surprised by all the young people in the cafés and pubs."

Silence.

"I wonder what percentage of Bamberg's population are students?" Adelle asked, hoping Tilly would take the bait.

"Twenty percent," Tilly said tersely.

"Almost twenty percent," Barbara said, still typing on her phone.

"Okay, Miss Smarty Pants," Tilly said, swiveling to face Barbara. "What percentage of the passengers on this ship have their university degree?"

Barbara looked up. "Extrapolating from the five of us, twenty percent."

Tilly crossed her arms. "Based on what?"

"I assume none of you has a degree," Barbara said. "One in five equals twenty percent."

Debbie laughed. "Based on what I know, at least sixty percent of us have degrees."

"Raise your hand if you have a degree," Tilly commanded. All five women raised their hands.

"Raise your hand if you have two degrees," Barbara ordered. Hers was the only hand in the air. Flicking her hair back, Barbara abruptly stood up and walked out.

Another topic to avoid, Adelle realized. Too late. Again.

Chapter Nine

Würzburg

"Barbara and Teresa took the optional tour to Rothenburg," Debbie announced at breakfast. "Teresa was excited to take the motor coach along the Romantic Road. It's supposed to be one of Bavaria's prettiest drives."

"I don't think Miss Two Degrees will find any romance," huffed Tilly. "Although I'm not so sure about Teresa. It depends on how many husbands went without their wives."

What? Adelle was shocked. But before she could challenge Tilly, her sister abruptly closed the topic.

"Tilly!" Debbie scolded. "That's enough!"

The morning was free for passengers to explore Würzburg on their own. Adelle joined Eileen and the physio group as they hiked through the impressive vineyards up to Marienberg Fortress, the old castle overlooking Würzburg. She was still getting over the shock of Tilly's accusation at breakfast. What was Tilly insinuating? Teresa couldn't possibly be hooking up with married men. *Could she?*

"You're deep in thought," Eileen observed.

Adelle decided to put her fears aside and enjoy the day. "I'm just admiring the view," she said, pointing down at the river. "Look, there's our ship."

The large and ornate Würzburg residence was overwhelming. The prince-bishops of Würzburg had started construction of the palace in 1719, and it had taken twenty-five years to complete. As Adelle ascended the elegant wide marble staircase, she stopped to admire the unsupported vaulted ceiling. It featured the largest ceiling fresco in the world, even larger than Michelangelo's at the Sistine Chapel. The artist had been commissioned to show how great Europe was, revolving around Würzburg as its center. Würzburg was surrounded by the rest of Europe, America, Africa, and Asia—the four known continents at the time.

Adelle chuckled at the portrayal of uncivilized America. The artist had painted a naked woman with feathers in her hair, sitting on an alligator amongst severed heads from a cannibal feast, being served what was said to be hot chocolate. Adelle had to stop herself from laughing out loud as she pictured herself serving morning hot chocolate to Barbara, sitting on an alligator.

Winding through the grandiose apartments, Adelle strolled behind Tilly and Vicki as they discussed the beautiful tapestries. Tilly dropped back to whisper to Adelle that

Rod had gone on the Rothenburg tour. Not wishing to gossip, Adelle had rushed ahead.

Adelle joined Debbie and Tilly as they sampled the local wine on the crowded old medieval bridge.

"Tilly, tell Adelle what you overheard," Debbie said, nudging her sister.

"I thought you didn't like it when I rubbernecked," Tilly said.

Debbie rolled her eyes and turned to Adelle. "Do you remember meeting "Mr. and Mrs. Wonderful" in the lounge?"

Adelle knew exactly who Debbie meant. How could she forget them! Especially Wilma, "Mrs. Wonderful." She had been flaunting the anniversary presents her husband had given her. They were the largest diamonds Adelle had ever seen, set in earrings, a ring, a bracelet, and a pendant necklace. Adelle nodded. Yes, she definitely remembered them.

"I met them the second day of our trip," Tilly scowled. "I was working on my quilt on the deck. Wilma paraded from couple to couple, showing off her anniversary diamonds." She wagged her finger at Adelle. "I don't like her. As our mother would say, she's too nice."

"They've spent a lot of time in the lounge after dinner," Debbie said. "At first, I noticed them every night, but I haven't seen them lately."

Adelle scanned her memory bank. "I don't think I've seen them since we switched ships."

"Me, neither," said Debbie. She set her wine glass down and turned to her sister. "Tilly, tell Adelle what you overheard."

"When we were swapping ships, Wilma's overnight bag went missing. Her husband insists he saw it lined up on the dock with the other luggage. It had a wide florescent orange strap, which made it easy to spot. But it didn't make it to their room in the new ship."

"That's unfortunate," Adelle said.

"There's more," Tilly said, pursing her lips. "Her jewelry and medication were in the missing bag."

"Her diamond jewelry!" Debbie cried.

"Apparently," Tilly reported, "she's more upset about her medication than her diamonds."

Both sisters were uncharacteristically quiet at the dinner table. Teresa was eating with people she had met on the Rothenburg tour, and Barbara was working in the cabin. Uncomfortable with the silence, Adelle brought up the missing jewelry.

"Funny you should mention that," Tilly said.

Debbie groaned. "I thought we agreed we wouldn't talk about it."

"She brought it up," Tilly said, gesturing at Adelle.

Adelle wondered what she had blundered into this time. Debbie stared at Tilly. Tilly glared back at Debbie.

"Tilly thinks a passenger on our ship stole the jewelry," Debbie finally said, breaking the standoff. "And she thinks she knows who."

Adelle was shocked. She found it hard to believe that one of the passengers took the diamonds. "Who, Tilly?"

"Teresa."

Teresa? "Our Teresa?" asked Adelle in disbelief. "Why would you say such a thing?"

"Her story doesn't add up. You said she was a kindergarten teacher. How can a kindergarten teacher afford to fly first class? And afford a stateroom all to herself? And Debbie said—"

"Don't bring me into this," Debbie cut in.

Tilly ignored her. "Debbie said she wears designer clothes and expensive pearls." Tilly crossed her arms. "And then there's the men ..."

"Tilly! I told you we weren't going to talk about this!" Debbie cried.

"What men?" Adelle asked.

Tilly's eyes narrowed. "Haven't you noticed her head-to-head conversations with every Tom, Dick, and Harry onboard? Debbie said—"

"Tilly ..." Debbie warned again.

"Debbie said that every night in the lounge, Teresa goes from man to man, talking up a storm. And don't forget about that room she has all to herself."

Stunned, Adelle turned to Debbie. "What do you think?" she asked.

Debbie sat there, staring at her plate.

Tilly leaned forward. "She thinks the thief is a different passenger. Tell her Debbie."

Debbie looked up, scowling. "It couldn't be Teresa. What about the person who disappears most of the time, who denies it when people have obviously seen her, who seems to be stalking everyone?"

Adelle's heart started to race.

"Barbara."

Adelle was grateful that Barbara wasn't in their stateroom when she returned after dinner. She needed to be by herself. This trip was turning into a disaster. Was one of the women a thief?

Tilly's evidence made sense. She had been right about Teresa flitting about from one man to another. She was certainly very outgoing. Adelle hadn't thought about her expensive wardrobe or accessories until Tilly had mentioned them. There had to be a reasonable explanation for her obvious wealth. Lottery winner? Beneficiary of a rich relative?

Crime?

Adelle recalled overhearing Teresa tell Rod that she was "tired of kindergarten" and was "looking for a man." What was that all about? But she was so nice!

Too nice?

Debbie's observations pointed to Barbara. Her behavior was definitely suspicious. She was so aloof and secretive. But Barbara wouldn't steal.

Would she?

Chapter Ten

Wertheim

The next morning, Adelle slipped out of her room without waking Barbara. She wasn't ready to face her just yet. She had worried much and slept little. Coffee. She needed coffee.

Lee was standing by the coffee station. Just the person she needed to talk to. After exchanging pleasantries, Adelle asked Lee to join her on the upper deck.

"I heard one of the passengers lost her medication and jewelry," Adelle said, trying to maintain a conversational tone.

Lee confirmed the news. "I took her to a pharmacist that same day and we were able to replace her medication," Lee said, frowning.

Adelle was relieved that the prescriptions were replaced.

"As for the missing jewelry, we don't know what happened," Lee confessed. "We had a security guard watching the luggage and nothing seemed amiss. We've never had anything like this happen before. It's a mystery."

Adelle joined the "easy" group for the walking tour of Wertheim. Their ship was docked alongside the medieval town center. It was a quaint, picturesque village and Bill was taking pictures every few steps. Their elderly guide was absolutely charming. He wore a heavy tweed jacket, with a wool scarf wrapped smartly around his neck. He gallantly tipped his fedora each time he passed one of the local women.

The guide entertained them with stories of Wertheim's colorful past. He described the early citizens as being very curious about one another. They didn't want their neighbors to know that they were watching them, so they built winding lanes, giving each snoopy person a better panoramic view. One homeowner must have been more than just curious. The guide pointed up at a small window. Its only purpose would have been to spy on the neighbors without being seen.

Who would go to that much trouble to spy on their neighbors? And why?

Their group stopped and gathered around an ancient lookout tower built near the river. It had also served as a prison. Legend had it that the townsfolk liked their peace and quiet. If two women were bickering and disturbing the peace, they were led up the very tall ladder to the only door in the tower. Then they were lowered by ropes to the inner ground floor. They were forced to stay together in the dark, sometimes for up to six weeks until they worked out their differences. Adelle grinned as she envisioned Debbie and

Tilly trying to resolve their issues in those circumstances. She bet it wouldn't take six weeks!

Adelle went up to the deck as the ship left the dock to sail through the scenic Tauber valley. She could hear her friends' laughter before she reached the top step.

"Adelle, just the person we were looking for," Debbie said, waving her over. She was sitting at one of the tables with Tilly and Teresa.

"What's so funny?" Adelle asked. Although she was happy to see the three of them together, she had a niggling feeling that something was up.

"Did your group hear the story about the lookout tower acting as a prison for grumpy women?" Debbie asked, grinning from ear to ear.

Tilly also seemed amused. Something was definitely up. "Yes, we did," Adelle replied. What was Teresa so smiley about?

"Tilly was in one group and I was in another," Debbie said. "Both of us realized what fools we were being. Life is too short to be mad at each other, so we went for coffee in the town square and talked it out."

"I saw them at the café and joined them," Teresa said. "I had no idea that Tilly was angry at me." She chuckled and looked at Tilly. "You were pretty blunt."

"Sorry." Tilly glanced at Debbie. "I didn't get any sleep last night."

"Me neither, sis," Debbie said, smiling at Tilly.

Teresa cleared her throat. "Tilly accused me of being a thief."

She did?

And yet, Teresa didn't seem upset. In fact, she was grinning.

"I know Tilly well enough by now," Teresa said, "that I assumed there must be a perfectly good reason for her accusation." She looked at Tilly. "Who told you I was a kindergarten teacher?"

Uh-oh.

Tilly pointed at Adelle. "She did."

"And who told you I was looking for a man?"

"She did," Tilly said, pointing at Adelle again.

Run!

Adelle knocked her deck chair over as she jumped to her feet and turned to flee.

"Adelle. Stop." Teresa grabbed Adelle's arm. "I'm not mad at you. In fact, we think it's pretty funny."

Funny?

Adelle heard a soft titter, followed by a louder giggle, followed by snorting. She opened her eyes. The girls couldn't contain themselves any longer and burst out laughing.

"It's okay, Adelle." Debbie said, wiping tears from her eyes. "We're not laughing at you, we're laughing with you."

Relieved, Adelle sat back down. She needed to explain herself.

"Teresa, when we were in Budapest I overheard you talking to Rod when I was walking around the ship's track."

"Were you rubbernecking?" Tilly asked with a chuckle.

Adelle felt her cheeks get hot. "Not intentionally."

"Teresa, you told Rod that you were tired of kindergarten," Adelle continued. "And later I heard you tell him that you needed a man." In a weak moment, Adelle had shared those tidbits with Tilly. That had been a mistake, she realized, looking at the older woman.

"Adelle spilled the beans and asked me not to tell," Tilly admitted. "But everyone knows I can't keep a secret. Right, Debbie?"

Debbie laughed. "They do now!"

"Teresa, I'm sorry I called you a floozy," Tilly said, between snorts of laughter.

"I must admit," Teresa said, chuckling, "that was a first."

"But you also have to admit that you've been spending an awful lot of time chatting with the men and not their wives," said Tilly. "Debbie said it happens every night in the lounge."

Debbie rolled her eyes.

"Guilty as charged," Teresa confessed. "I'm not a kindergarten teacher. Lately though, I've felt like one. I own a construction company. We just finished a large project and we're waiting to start the next one. My team is restless so they horse around a lot in the office. It seems like I'm always trying to get them to settle down."

That made sense. "What about 'needing a man?'" Adelle asked, curious.

Teresa seemed puzzled for a moment and then she smiled. "That must have been when I was explaining to Rod that I need a man, or woman for that matter, to replace the key head supervisor who is retiring."

"And all the one-on-one conversations with the husbands?" Tilly asked.

Teresa took longer to respond. Finally, she sighed deeply. "To be honest, I've forgotten how to be comfortable around women. I mostly work with men." The corners of Teresa's mouth slowly turned up.

"I don't cook," Teresa said, grinning at Adelle. "I don't sew," she informed Tilly. "And I have a personal shopper do all my wardrobe buying," she told Debbie.

There was a brief silence while everyone digested Teresa's revelations.

"What about opera?" Adelle asked.

Teresa burst out laughing. "What gave you the idea I like opera?"

"In Budapest, you went back to the Opera House in your free time," Adelle answered sheepishly. Then she had a thought. "You said you were in the construction industry. Is that why? To look at the building?"

"Yes!" exclaimed Teresa. "Our son joined the business shortly after my husband passed away five years ago. He's an architect. It was his idea that I get out of the office for a break so he arranged this river cruise vacation for me. Before I left, he told me about his interest in European architecture." She looked pointedly at Adelle. "Rod has the same passion for architectural detail." Her lips turned up and she raised one eyebrow. "It's obvious you don't."

Guilty as charged. Adelle apologized.

"That's okay," Teresa said. "It's not for everyone." She turned to Tilly. "While we're clearing the air, I want to apologize for all the questions about dementia and senior care options. Maria Theresa Habsburg really inspired me. Even though I promised my son I wouldn't work on this trip, I've been thinking about building active senior residences and communities."

A chorus of "hellos" from shore interrupted the conversation as a group of cyclists rode by. Adelle realized it must be the optional tour group who were biking the five hours from Wertheim to Freudenberg.

Was that Barbara in the middle of the group?

Chapter Eleven

Koblenz

Adelle woke with a start. She had been dreaming about kings and queens, and knights in shining armor. Why were the knights moaning? *Wait a minute.* The moaning was in her stateroom.

"Barbara, are you okay?" Adelle asked.

"I'm a little stiff and sore," Barbara replied in the darkness.

Adelle took a moment to fully wake up, slowly recalling the previous afternoon. When Barbara returned from the bike tour, she looked exhausted. She had hobbled into their cabin and flopped down face-first on her bed. "I won't be at dinner," she had mumbled.

Wide awake now, Adelle debated if it was time to engage Barbara in conversation. Come on, she told herself. You can do this. Talk to Barbara. She's moaning, she's human, she won't bite. Hopefully.

Don't be ridiculous, Adelle. Time to be a big girl.

Adelle smiled. She had often told her granddaughter it was time to be a big girl. Taking a deep breath, Adelle spoke into the darkness. "I heard that was a five-hour bike ride yesterday."

"Four hours and thirty-three minutes."

Adelle rolled her eyes. Did Barbara always have to be so precise? She tried again. "How long has it been since you rode a bike?"

"Fifteen years, three months, and seven days," Barbara finally replied.

For goodness' sake! Adelle tried not to sound exasperated. "Since?"

"The last day of high school."

"Why did it take you so long to ride again?" And so far, Adelle wondered to herself.

"My bike was stolen."

Although Adelle felt sorry for Barbara, she was happy that they were finally having a conversation. Even if it was in the dark.

"What are your plans for today?" Adelle asked.

"Work."

Adelle scrambled to think up another open-ended question. Time to notch it up a bit. "What are you working on?"

"You wouldn't understand," Barbara snapped in the darkness.

Adelle lost her courage. Time to quit asking questions.

"Adelle?" Barbara whimpered after another long silence.

"Yes?" Adelle perked up. Maybe Barbara was going to tell her about her work after all.

"Muffins and fruit with coffee this morning?" Barbara moaned. "Please?"

Adelle bumped into Lee at the coffee station as she assembled muffins and fruit. "For Barbara?" Lee guessed, steadying Adelle's tray for her.

"Yes, how did you know?"

"It took her awhile to walk up the gangplank after her ride yesterday," Lee replied. "And then she switched her trip from the 'demanding' castle tour to the 'easy' fortress tour." Lee grinned. "Between you and me, she was relatively pleasant compared to when we first met."

"What do you mean?" Adelle asked, remembering her own first impression of Barbara.

"She expected me to answer all her questions about the other passengers. Where they were from, what cabin they were in, etcetera. Of course, I couldn't help her. Those details are protected by privacy policies."

And they're none of her business, thought Adelle. What a strange young woman.

Lee held Adelle's tray while she carefully prepared Barbara's coffee: one-third regular, two-thirds decaf, and lots of hot milk. "By the way, if you're going to Marksburg Castle, you may want to ride in the front of the bus. It's a very winding road."

Once again, Adelle was grateful for Lee's attention to detail. He had remembered her problem with motion sickness. Thankfully, river cruising didn't bother her, but long winding roads posed a problem. She blinked and looked up, trying to stop her tears. It was so embarrassing. After retiring, she was prone to tearing up whenever anyone was nice to her. She smiled as she remembered what her grand-daughter had told her. "It's okay, Grandma. It's just your heart coming out your eyes."

After delivering breakfast to Barbara, Adelle mulled over Lee's comments. Why was Barbara so inquisitive about the other passengers? What work was she doing? Was Debbie right? Her stomach clenched.

Time to contact Maureen.

Logging in to the ship's computer in the library, Adelle felt badly about letting her granddaughter down. She had resolved to limit her screen time. Scrolling down her inbox, she noticed two emails from Maureen. She read the latest one, from a few days ago:

"Glad to hear things are peachy. Enjoy the trip."

Peachy? Why would Maureen say that?

Barbara.

Adelle had a vivid memory of Barbara working on her laptop and then looking up to ask Adelle if everything was okay. Adelle wasn't okay. At the time, she was worried about the looming ship swap. "Just peachy," she had replied.

Was Barbara spying on her for Maureen?

Don't be ridiculous, Adelle! She clicked on the first email from Maureen, noticing that it had been sent on the day they started their trip in Budapest.

"Thanks again for hosting for me," Maureen's email said. "I wouldn't trust this assignment to anyone else. Sorry I couldn't brief you in person. Take good care of Teresa—she is a very successful businesswoman and has the potential to be my best client."

Uh-oh. If only I had known that earlier.

Adelle continued reading.

"Tilly is one of my best referral sources. I hope to arrange more group trips for women traveling solo."

More trips? Adelle grinned at the prospect.

"As for my niece Barbara …"

Niece?!

"… please help, as her reputation is at stake. Desperate people do desperate things."

What did Maureen mean? Adelle worried, dropping into the front seat of the motor coach. Did she think that for some reason her niece was desperate enough to steal? Too late, Adelle realized that she was sitting beside Dorothy, the annoying video lady. "No videoing today?" Adelle asked hopefully, after introductions.

"Not until we get to the castle itself," Dorothy replied. "I've heard that the road winds back and forth and I'm afraid it will make my friend back home nauseous."

"Your friend back home?" Adelle asked. She caught herself wondering how anyone so annoying could have friends.

"She couldn't come. Between the booking and departure dates, she was diagnosed with a serious illness and had to cancel. I plan on sharing every detail of this trip with her when I get back."

Adelle felt ashamed. She had assumed Dorothy was selfish and inconsiderate. Again, she had jumped to the wrong conclusion. When would she ever learn?

The walking path from the parking lot to Marksburg Castle was steep. Adelle carefully picked her way over the large uneven boulders up the inclined entry tunnel. She could see why this excursion was labeled demanding. She was glad Tilly had opted for the easier tour to the Ehrenbreitstein Fortress. Even hiking boots were no match for this difficult terrain.

The spectacular view of the Rhine and the surrounding towns was well worth the climb. Adelle stood to one side to let Dorothy video the beautiful scenery below. Their guide informed them that despite being there for over eight hundred years, this was the only castle on the Rhine that had never been destroyed. Now it was owned and operated by the German Castle Association.

Adelle was fascinated by the exhibits, including the wine cellar and the gothic kitchen with an oven big enough to roast a whole ox. The short beds allowed their occupants to sleep sitting up, likely necessary due to chronic breathing problems caused by constant exposure to fireplace smoke.

Adelle and Dorothy laughed when they saw the medieval privy. Instead of using chamber pots, there was an upstairs outhouse, a tiny room that stuck out from the side of the building. It was strategically positioned. Over a pig sty!

The old horse stables featured another surprise, a small exhibition about torture and punishment in the Middle Ages. Seeing the rack, she imagined stiff and sore Barbara enjoying a good stretch. Her smile was short-lived. Maybe Barbara was a thief and deserved to be tortured.

Adelle, I can't believe you are thinking like this. Enough!

Adelle made her decision. It was time to confront Barbara.

Adelle heard her name being called and looked up as Tilly hurried into the lounge.

"Adelle, Debbie … there you are," Tilly said, trying to catch her breath. "Barbara hurt her ankle." Tilly motioned to Bill and Eileen who were supporting a very pale Barbara as she limped into the lounge.

Adelle jumped into action. She pulled out a chair for Barbara and then rushed to the bar to get ice and a towel. When she returned, Bill was gently examining Barbara's ankle.

"I think she just twisted it a bit," Bill said.

Tilly looked puzzled. "He said she needs rice."

Eileen grinned. "Let me translate. RICE stands for Rest, Ice, Compression, and Elevation."

"I can't rest now," Barbara moaned, dropping her head into her hands. "Not when I'm so close."

So close to what? wondered Adelle.

Bill left to get a tensor bandage just as Teresa arrived. "What's going on?" she asked.

"Tilly was just about to fill us in," Debbie said, turning to her sister. "From the beginning."

"Barbara and I were in the same cable car going up to the fortress. When we got there, she was stiff and having trouble walking, so I suggested we sit and have coffee." Tilly jabbed her finger into Debbie's shoulder. "I asked her."

"Asked her what?" demanded Debbie.

"If she was a thief," Tilly replied.

For goodness' sake! Tilly was always so direct. Adelle realized that was what she really appreciated about her. She always knew where she was coming from.

"Guess what?" Tilly asked. "She didn't know anything about the missing jewelry and medication!"

Unless she was lying.

"Were you gossiping again?" Debbie asked.

"I was sharing news," Tilly replied, thrusting out her chin. "She asked me to describe the jewelry. Then she got all worked up."

"Barbara, what is going on?" Adelle demanded, hands on her hips. Time to be like Tilly.

Barbara glanced around the lounge and then looked up at Adelle, eyes pleading. "I can't talk here."

At Adelle's request, the women helped Barbara back to their cabin. As Adelle and Teresa used pillows to prop her ankle up, Debbie turned to Tilly. "What happened after you gossiped about the diamonds?"

Tilly shrugged. "I may as well have been invisible. Barbara spent the rest of the time tapping on her phone. When the motor coach brought us back to the ship, she tripped getting off." Tilly wagged her finger at Barbara. "You were looking at your phone instead of watching where you were going."

"It's not polite to point," Barbara said weakly.

Time to take charge, Adelle.

"Barbara, what is going on? I'm not backing down this time."

Barbara stared at Adelle. Adelle stared back.

"I was checking to see if a claim had been filed," Barbara finally said.

"For what?" Adelle asked.

"Earrings, a ring, a bracelet, and a pendant. All big diamonds. They were insured for almost a million dollars."

Adelle's legs felt weak. "Was a claim filed?" she asked, propping herself up against the wall.

Barbara briefly smiled. "Affirmative."

Suddenly, it all came together. Adelle started to tingle. "The work you've been doing—would it have anything to do with insurance fraud?"

"Yes."

So that's why she's been following everyone, Adelle realized. Could Mr. and Mrs. Wonderful have faked the theft of the overnight case? Wilma's husband said he saw it waiting to be loaded.

Adelle had an idea. She rushed to the lounge and found Dorothy, the video lady. Her suspicions were confirmed. Mr. Wonderful had lied. Adelle spoke quickly with Lee and rushed back to brief the women.

"Lee told me that the ship had a security guard watching the luggage on shore before it was put onto the transport truck. Everything was accounted for as it was loaded, unloaded, and then placed in each passenger's stateroom." Adelle was grateful that Dorothy was so detailed. "The overnight bag never was there. We have video proof."

"What about the missing medications?" Tilly asked.

"Lee personally accompanied Wilma into town that afternoon and they were replaced," Adelle replied. "But she didn't tell anyone that."

"Of course not," Teresa said, rubbing her chin. "The missing medication was a decoy. Everyone worried about her medication and felt sorry for her instead of focusing on the missing jewelry."

"Poor Lee," Adelle said. "They've been insinuating a staff member stole the missing diamonds and they've insisted on special treatment, including complimentary tours. Now they've demanded a private car to take them to Germany's top Michelin-ranked restaurant. Tonight."

Debbie snapped her fingers. "She wants to show off the jewelry one last time, away from the ship. She's going to flaunt the diamonds tonight! I just know it!"

"Would they take the risk that other passengers might be there and see them?" Teresa asked.

"I thought about that, too," Adelle replied. "Lee said the restaurant is over an hour's drive from here. We checked, just in case. No other passengers have reservations there tonight."

"From what Debbie told me," Tilly said, "Wilma likes attention and the spotlight." She glanced sideways at her sister. "Debbie's right. She'll wear all of it tonight."

Everyone started to talk at the same time. Before Adelle could get their attention again, Barbara tried to stand up, but collapsed back onto her bed in obvious pain.

"Where do you think you're going, young lady?" Tilly demanded.

Barbara moaned. "It's my last chance. I have to follow them and take a picture of them with the diamonds. Otherwise, I'm ruined." She started to cry. "And so is my mother."

Barbara faced ruin? And her mother?

Adelle decided to ask more questions later. Right now, there was no time to lose.

Think, Adelle, think. She had a brainwave.

"Girls, we don't have much time. It's almost five o'clock. Their car is booked for five forty-five, and their reservation is at seven o'clock."

The cabin went quiet.

"Barbara, have you brought disguises?" Adelle asked, suddenly remembering the woman sitting behind the physios at the cathedral in Passau.

"Yes," Barbara said, wiping at her tears.

"Wigs?" Adelle asked.

"Affirmative."

It was all starting to make sense. Barbara kept all of her outfits in the big suitcase. Only Adelle's clothes were hanging in their closet. Adelle had never seen Barbara get dressed and had chalked it up to modesty.

Teresa agreed to go to the restaurant with Adelle, and left to get changed. Debbie agreed to put together a disguise for Adelle while she went to make their reservation and book a car.

When Adelle returned, clothes, accessories, and wigs were flung everywhere. Teresa was already dressed in an elegant black dress and black shawl, sporting large-framed glasses.

"Barbara's shawl?" Adelle inquired.

"Mine," Teresa answered, as Debbie adjusted the black wig to cover Teresa's auburn hair. "I always carry it with me. Just in case. The wig and glasses belong to Barbara."

The wig from Passau, Adelle realized.

Debbie was clearly in her element, merrily throwing clothes at Adelle. "Quick, this skirt has an elastic waistband. I think it will fit. And try this long tunic over it. And this wig."

"Barbara's clothes will never fit me," Adelle wailed.

"Don't worry," Barbara said. "I packed a larger outfit for my Aunt Maureen." She smirked. "Just in case."

"I'll go stand near the exit ramp, Tilly said. "Just in case the Wonderfuls are early."

Barbara handed her phone to Adelle. "It's charged and ready to go. Get as many photos as you can."

Debbie slowly opened the door and looked both ways. "The coast is clear." She turned back and winked. "I'll go first. Just in case."

When Adelle peered into the reception area near the ramp, she held her breath. Tilly and Debbie were talking to Mr. and Mrs. Wonderful, who were facing away from the exit.

"You poor dear," Adelle overheard Tilly say as she and Teresa slipped by. "I heard you lost your medications. What do you take? Maybe I can …"

Adelle had just settled into her seat in the upscale restaurant when Teresa suddenly lifted her menu in front of her face. "They're here!" she whispered.

Adelle's stomach clenched and her heart started to race. She started to count her breaths.

One, two …

"Relax," Teresa murmured.

If it was only that simple!

"What are they doing now?" Adelle quietly asked.

"The staff are making a big fuss over Wilma. I can see the diamonds sparkling from here."

Adelle rolled her shoulders as she scanned her menu.

For goodness' sake! The feature was a ten-course dinner and would cost her a whole month's pension!

One, two …

"They're making a big production of tasting the wine," Teresa reported, rolling her eyes. She watched them for another minute. "No surprise. It's not good enough. Now the wine steward is scampering away for another bottle."

Adelle winced. "The cruise line is paying. They'll probably order the most expensive wine in the cellar."

Adelle fought against the urge to run over, snap the incriminating pictures, and run out to their waiting car. Teresa must have sensed her anxiety and distracted Adelle with a lesson on good wines.

"Producing   quality   wine   requires   patience," Teresa concluded.

Point taken, thought Adelle.

"Here she comes." Teresa ducked her head and rustled around in her purse. Adelle held her breath. Wilma walked past them on her way to the restroom, unaware of the cell phone peeking out of Teresa's bag.

"I got the ring," Teresa murmured as she quickly scanned her photos. She passed the phone to Adelle. "Your turn. I'll distract Wilma on her way back."

Adelle dipped her chin slightly. On cue, Teresa reached out and pointed to the window on the far wall. As Wilma turned her head to see what Teresa was pointing at, Adelle held the photo button down, taking multiple pictures until Wilma turned forward again.

Breathe, Adelle, breathe. She dropped the phone quietly onto her lap, bowed her head, and concentrated on keeping her hands from shaking while she cut her food into tiny pieces.

Wilma passed by.

Phew!

Adelle saw Debbie, Tilly, Barbara, and Lee waiting at the entranceway as she and Teresa crossed the ramp onto the ship.

"Success?" Barbara asked nervously.

"Affirmative," Adelle said, handing Barbara her phone.

Barbara quickly swiped through the photos.

"Bingo."

Chapter Twelve

Cologne

Was that coffee Adelle could smell? She rolled onto her back and stretched out under the covers. Then she opened her eyes. Barbara was sitting on the edge of the bed, holding two steaming cups of coffee.

"Good morning," Barbara said, smiling broadly.

Adelle felt like pinching herself. Was she dreaming?

"Regular with a little cream," Barbara said, passing her a cup.

"Thanks." Adelle wriggled up against her headboard and savored her first sip. "How's your ankle this morning?"

"Functional," Barbara replied.

The advantage of being young, thought Adelle. Then she remembered the previous night and sat straight up, nearly spilling her coffee. "What time is it? Have you met with the Wonderfuls yet?"

Barbara looked at her phone. "Eight twenty-seven." She looked up and grinned. "Yes."

The previous night, Lee was waiting for Wilma and her husband when they staggered up the ramp to the ship. They had the nerve to present receipts for their expenses for the evening and had demanded immediate reimbursement. Watching from a distance, Adelle admired Lee's restraint. He told them he would meet them at 7:30 the next morning to do the necessary paperwork.

Adelle tried not to show her impatience. "What happened?"

"The ship's captain joined Lee and me at 7:20. The fraudsters arrived at 7:46. Late. When we showed them the incriminating photos, they admitted their role in the organized insurance fraud scheme."

Organized? Adelle gripped her coffee cup with both hands.

"What do you mean by organized?"

"The diamonds are real. There is a crime ring that passes them from one insurance claimant to another."

Adelle took several deep breaths. *The ship swap.* It had been the perfect opportunity to stage the disappearance.

Barbara continued. "The fraudsters knew they were caught and were willing to cooperate. They named names. And they handed over the jewelry."

"What will happen to them?" Adelle asked, purely out of curiosity. She didn't feel sorry for them.

"All I can tell you is that they've left the cruise." Barbara's eyes crinkled and she smiled.

"What's so amusing?" Adelle asked.

"They will be billed for the optional tours they demanded. And they won't be reimbursed for last night's expenses."

Ouch, thought Adelle. The car was expensive and the restaurant bill would have been astronomical.

Barbara grinned.

"What else, Barbara?"

"The cruise line is very grateful. All of our expenses will be reimbursed."

Barbara put down her coffee. "Lee is meeting our group for breakfast," she said, opening her laptop. "You have time to dress while I finish my report."

So much for a leisurely coffee.

Lee was sitting with Debbie, Tilly, and Teresa at their usual breakfast table. "Good morning," he said cheerfully. "I can't stay long, but I have a pleasant duty to perform." Their server arrived with a tray of mimosas and Lee passed them around. "On behalf of the captain and our cruise line, I would like to salute all of you for your good work." He stood and raised his glass. "Cheers!"

As they clinked their glasses and sampled their mimosas, Adelle saw Ann toasting her from across the room. Morning mimosas on vacation didn't seem so bad after all.

Lee sat down and smiled. "To thank you, we would like to treat your group to a private tour of Cologne tonight," Lee announced. "We'll visit local brew houses to sample Kolsch, and then we'll have dinner at a famous brauhaus."

"What's Kolsch?" Debbie asked.

"I know," Tilly answered, eyes twinkling. "It's a light, crisp beer brewed only here in Cologne. They serve it cold, straight from the barrel."

"How do you know that, sis?"

Tilly chuckled. "When you're out partying all night, I read the ship's daily newsletters." She turned to Adelle and winked. "Someone has to know what's going on."

Adelle laughed, raising her mimosa in salute.

Lee thanked them one more time before he left. "Enjoy your tour of Cologne this morning, and make sure you rest up this afternoon. Tonight, we're going to celebrate!"

Debbie clicked her pink fingernails against her mimosa flute. "Barbara, what have you been up to?"

"It's confidential."

"We promise not to tell anyone, right Tilly?" Debbie said, nudging her sister.

Tilly shrugged her shoulders.

Barbara pursed her lips and then put down her glass. "I can share some information."

At last, thought Adelle, all ears.

"I work for a major insurance firm. Insurance companies share data to help detect and prevent fraud. Analyzing the claims data, I noticed a pattern."

"Go on," Teresa said, paying rapt attention.

"Multiple claims have been filed in the past six months for diamond jewelry, specifically earrings, a ring, a bracelet, and a pendant. The other major river cruise lines were targeted."

"It was our turn," Tilly guessed.

"That's what the data suggested," Barbara said. "Your travel agent, Maureen, is my aunt. I booked this trip through her, deducing that I would be on the right ship at the right time."

"It must have caught you off guard when you arrived and found me instead of your aunt," Adelle said, remembering with a cringe how upset Barbara had been.

"I don't like surprises," Barbara admitted.

Teresa turned to Barbara. "How did you narrow it down to this trip?"

"You wouldn't understand," Barbara answered.

"Try us," Teresa challenged.

"Give us a chance," Tilly chimed in.

Barbara shifted in her chair. Pressing her fingertips together, she launched into the details.

Adelle heard "… predictive analytics … statistical modeling … randomized algorithms." She didn't understand any of it. Her attention drifted until she heard "background checks" and "social media."

Aha, this must be what Barbara was doing on her computer each day. Adelle thought she had been texting with her friends.

Although Teresa was leaning forward, fixated on Barbara's every word, Tilly's eyes were glazing over and Debbie was refolding her napkin. *A swan! How does she do that?*

"Adelle," Teresa said, "I was just asking Barbara what led her into the field of insurance fraud."

Adelle tried her best to focus. Barbara had obtained degrees in criminal justice and sociology, with many advanced computer classes. She had interned with a major insurance company and had been promoted to the Special Investigations Unit.

"This case is very important," Barbara said. "I developed an innovative predictions model and I wanted to test its reliability."

Adelle recalled Maureen's email about Barbara's reputation and desperation. More things were starting to make sense. But not everything. "Why were you worried that you and your mother would be ruined?"

Barbara looked down at her plate. "I used vacation time and a loan from my mother to be here." Then she looked up and grinned. "Now my costs will be covered."

"Barbara," said Teresa, "I think I understand your methodology. Can you explain what you do in a simpler way?"

"I'll try. You're all familiar with the concept of who, what, when, where, why, and how, right?" Everyone nodded and gave Barbara their full attention. "I knew the what—diamond jewelry. When? The pattern indicated this month. Where? Likely on this cruise line. Why? It was the only major line not yet victimized. How? I wasn't sure."

"What about 'who?'" Tilly asked. "You forgot about 'who.'"

Barbara frowned. "That was the most difficult variable."

"You didn't think it was any of us, did you?" Debbie asked.

"Each of you was at the top of my list. Starting with Adelle."

Ouch!

After Barbara had overhead Adelle thank Lee for being her alibi, Barbara couldn't rule out either one of them. The girls all laughed when a red-faced Adelle explained meeting with Lee as her excuse for avoiding shopping the first day.

"Why did you suspect the rest of us?" Tilly asked.

"I had to start somewhere," Barbara replied. "After methodically eliminating each of you as suspects, I focused on your new friends."

"Why?" asked Teresa.

"Privacy issues. I couldn't obtain any information about the other passengers. I had to learn their names and find out more details myself."

So that's why she was following people.

Barbara grinned at Tilly. "I learned how to rubberneck from you. I noticed that people ignored you when you were working on your fidget quilt. Being occupied with my phone worked the same way."

Adelle walked beside Vicki as their group toured the famous Cologne cathedral. Teresa and Rod were deep in conversation about its gothic features.

"Better Teresa than me," Vicki said, gently elbowing Adelle in the ribs.

Adelle laughed. "Better Rod than me."

Construction of the cathedral had started in 1248 and had continued in several stages over the next seven centuries. "Thankfully the cathedral wasn't completely destroyed in World War II," the guide said. "The double spires served as navigational landmarks and saved the building from being totally flattened like the rest of the city."

As they walked through Cologne, Adelle chuckled at some of the cheeky sculpture art. On the wall of one tavern, she couldn't help laugh out loud at a sculpture of a monk carrying a tipsy young man on his shoulders.

Their guide pointed up to the clock on the town hall tower. Beneath the clock, Adelle saw a wooden sculpture of a man's grotesque face. When the clock struck the hour, the figure stuck out its tongue!

"Who is that young lady walking beside Tilly?" Vicki asked. "I don't think I've met her yet."

But she knows who you are.

Time to introduce Barbara to the rest of the passengers.

After a lively lunch, everyone scattered when Teresa asked Barbara if she could explain more about her innovative work and use of data analysis.

"I'm going for a nap," Tilly said, yawning.

Debbie jumped up from the table. "I'm going shopping with Ann."

Adelle noticed that Barbara was settling in for a long lecture. Tilly had a good idea. Time for a nap.

The beer tour was so much fun! Adelle had needlessly worried that they would drink too much beer from over-sized steins.

"These are kid-sized glasses," Tilly grumbled as their server brought their first beer.

Lee chuckled. "To make sure the beer is always cold and fresh, remember? Don't worry, the servers will keep the beer flowing." He reminded them that they were going to tour two other breweries before dinner. "You might want to pace yourselves," he suggested. "The server will keep bringing you another full glass until you cover your empty one with your coaster."

Tilly raised her glass. "Post!" she exclaimed.

"Oh, Tilly," Debbie said. "It's *prost*. With an r."

"Same thing only different," Teresa said, laughing as she raised her glass.

Back onboard after their tour of the breweries and dinner, Lee suggested they proceed to the lounge. Teresa seized Barbara's elbow and Adelle followed her lead, grabbing Tilly's arm. "Come on, Tilly. It's time you found out what the night owls do!"

The regulars were still in the lounge when they arrived. Adelle waved at Bill and Eileen, seated with the other physios.

"Hi Tilly," Ann said. "I hope you're here to keep your sister, Teresa, and Adelle under control." She turned to Barbara, offering her hand. "We haven't met. I'm Ann."

To Adelle's surprise, Barbara smiled warmly as she shook Ann's hand. "I'm Barbara, but my friends call me Barb."

Tilly stared at Barbara and then extended her hand. "Nice to meet you. Barb."

There was an awkward silence. Then Adelle grinned, Teresa snickered, Debbie giggled, and Tilly laughed so hard she started to snort.

Chapter Thirteen

Kinderdijk

Adelle woke with a start. Had she heard dogs barking? Silence. She drifted off to sleep again. The next time she stirred, she thought she heard whimpering. Had she been whimpering and woken herself up?

Adelle slowly opened her eyes. The cabin was pitch black. She turned her head from side to side. Good. No headache. Then she grinned as the previous evening's celebration came back to her.

The brewery tours were interesting and the traditional German dinner was good, but the highlight of the night had definitely been partying together in the lounge afterwards. Tilly and Barbara ended up declaring themselves best friends forever. Adelle grinned, remembering tiny Tilly with her arms stretched up to Barbara's shoulders, teaching her how to do the Beer Barrel Polka. Later, Debbie had led all the lounge guests in a boisterous conga line dance. When Teresa had told Tilly it was midnight, Tilly had stuck out her tongue! Adelle jokingly suggested that Debbie might have to carry her sister back to their room, just like the sculpture of the monk. Hearing that, Tilly had insisted that she was perfectly capable of finding their cabin herself. To everyone's amusement, she had curtsied, twirled around, and skipped out of the lounge.

Another Tilly classic.

Music brought Adelle back to the present. It was the despised "Blue Danube Waltz." This time, Adelle knew she wasn't dreaming. What was going on?

"Barbara …?"

"It's Barb."

Adelle heard Barb rustling in her bed in the darkness. "Do you hear music?"

"Yes."

"Where is it coming from?"

Barb moaned. "My phone," she said.

Adelle lay still, a thought slowly creeping into her brain. "Have you been hitting the snooze button?"

"Affirmative."

"Have you programmed your own alarm sounds?"

"Yes."

Open-ended questions, Adelle. When will you ever learn? "What sounds?"

"Barking dogs, the 'Blue Danube Waltz,' whimpering dogs. Whatever will annoy me enough to get up and turn it off."

Adelle was relieved that she wasn't going crazy after all. Her thoughts returned to the previous night. Barb had become more and more animated and had eventually revealed that she had moved back home to support her recently widowed mother.

Suddenly, Adelle had an epiphany.

"Barb?"

"Yes?"

"By any chance, does your mother bring you coffee every morning?"

"It's how we start our day."

That explains the morning coffee ritual, Adelle realized. And here she had resented providing room service when Barb was simply seeking the comforting routines of home. With a sinking feeling, it occurred to Adelle that the baggy gray sweatshirt had likely belonged to Barb's late father.

Adelle threw her covers off. It was her turn to get coffee.

Adelle couldn't believe that this was their last day on the river cruise. Two weeks had gone by much too quickly. As she strolled around the walking track on the top deck, she noticed the other passengers enjoying the warm autumn sunshine. Tilly was sitting in a deck chair, working on her fidget quilt. Barb was sitting beside her, "studying human behavior" as she listened to country music through her earbuds. Debbie was laughing with Ann and Joe. Bill was leaning on the railing, taking pictures of the idyllic countryside. Teresa, Vicki, and Rod were visiting by the captain's wheelhouse.

"May I join you?" Eileen asked cheerfully.

Adelle was delighted to see her friend. "Of course!"

"Congratulations," Eileen said. "I heard Mr. and Mrs. Wonderful got the justice they deserved."

Adelle stopped mid-step. Barb had asked everyone not to say anything. She wondered what Eileen knew.

"Don't worry," said Eileen. "We know it's hush-hush. Last night, Tilly told us they were caught red-handed with the missing jewelry. She said it was top secret. We promised her we wouldn't tell anyone."

Time to change the topic.

"Do you notice how happy and content everyone looks?" Adelle asked, continuing the walk. Eileen agreed.

After another lap, Adelle chuckled as they passed Teresa and the Aussies again.

"What's so funny?" Eileen asked.

"I was thinking about the last two weeks. When Maureen asked me to host this group, I was so grateful. Somebody needed me. Then I found out that the cruise line took care of all the details. There was nothing for me to do."

"Isn't that the idea of a vacation?" Eileen asked.

"Yes, I suppose so. But I guess I've always been driven by goals, so I set a goal to make the girls happy."

"How did that work out?"

"It was a disaster. I made so many wrong assumptions and everything seemed to backfire."

Adelle really appreciated her new friend. Eileen was such a good listener. Adelle felt free to think out loud without being judged. "The harder I tried, the worse things got. And then I tried something different."

"What was that?" Eileen asked.

"I quit trying."

"To make everyone happy?"

"Yes." Adelle stopped walking and turned to Eileen. "Tilly taught me that. She works hard to stay healthy, but she doesn't try to make everyone else healthy." *Not directly*, she thought to herself. "Even though I would like everyone to be happy and healthy, it's not my job. Each person is responsible for her own life. I can't make anyone happy any more than I can make them exercise, eat properly, or get enough sleep."

Adelle chuckled again. "I've learned that happiness is an inside job."

Adelle enjoyed the leisurely pace of their afternoon tour of Kinderdijk. She learned about its network of windmills and other methods used to manage floods. Their ingenuity had earned them UNESCO world heritage site status in 1997. Another check for Rod.

"It's so peaceful here," Debbie remarked. "The gentle wind, the flowing water, the whirring of the windmills."

Adelle imagined what it must have been like to raise a family inside the living quarters of the windmill. Before electricity. The area was small, but big enough for beds for the children and parents, and a small kitchen and eating area. Adelle wound her way up the stairs to the apparatus above. It was fascinating to learn how the windmills worked.

"What a picturesque stop," marveled Bill later as he passed his digital camera around, letting people in their group view his photos. His pictures were stunning. When asked, he agreed to share his photos by email.

Email.

Adelle made a mental note to log in when they got back to the ship. A professional tour host would confirm flights.

For their farewell dinner, the chef had prepared a special meal to celebrate wonderful memories and newfound friends.

"It's too hard to choose," Debbie whined, looking at the menu. "I want to order everything."

Adelle agreed. "I have an idea," she said, putting her menu down.

"Of course, you do," Debbie said brightly, and all the women laughed.

Tilly snorted. "If we give you a minute, you'll probably forget it and come up with another one."

Adelle joined the laughter. "Busted. But before I forget, why don't we order one or two of everything? Then we can pass it around and eat family style."

For starters, they shared salmon tartar salad, tomato salad with crisp tandoori chicken and parmesan foam, and roasted forest mushrooms. Then they each savored several helpings of the pumpkin mousse ravioli with lamb loin.

Debbie elbowed Tilly. "I'll bet our husbands are tired of canned beans by now."

Tilly chuckled. "And cheese sandwiches."

Adelle was definitely going to miss the delicious meals. And her new girlfriends.

"Adelle, are your allergies bothering you again?" Teresa asked her quietly as Barb and the sisters traded home-cooking stories.

Adelle took a moment to compose herself. "I was just thinking how much I'm going to miss everyone. We'll probably never see each other again."

Teresa's eyes misted. "I know how you feel."

Suddenly Teresa sat up and clapped her hands for attention. "Girls," she cried. "We should plan another trip together!"

Silence.

Then everyone started to talk at once.

"Marie Antoinette went to Paris. I want to see Paris," Tilly said, thrusting out her chin.

Debbie looked at her sister. "It's my turn to plan our next trip. How about another river cruise?"

"Starting in Paris," insisted Tilly. "I've been reading the brochures …"

"And I've been chatting with the other passengers …" Teresa said. Everyone burst out laughing again.

"We noticed," Tilly said.

Teresa grinned. "Guilty as charged. A number of them raved about cruising in the Provence region … castles, wine-tasting, French cuisine …"

"I know a good tour host," Barb said.

Adelle held her breath.

Barb looked around the table, and then raised her wine glass.

"To Adelle, the best tour host ever!"

CPSIA information can be obtained
at www.ICGtesting.com
Printed in the USA
LVHW111456060821
694724LV00002B/52